To: MATThew,

Good Reading!! Remember IT'S
ONly fICTION — OR IS IT ?

THE
CONVERSION
PROPHECY

Best Wishes,

[signature]

THE
CONVERSION
PROPHECY

MICHAEL SOLOMON

Green Dragon Books
Palm Beach, FL
USA

The Conversion Prophecy

A Green Dragon Publishing Group Publication

Green Dragon Publishing
P.O. Box 1608
Lake Worth, FL 33460

http://www.greendragonbooks.com

info@greendragonbooks.com

Printed in the United States of America and the United Kingdom

ISBN (Paperback) 978-1-62386-013-4

ISBN (Hardcover) 978-1-62386-015-8

ISBN (e-book) 978-1-62386-014-1

Library of Congress Cataloging-in-Publication Data Control # 2015936060

For

Sydney, Max, Isabella, and Harley,

Who give me true joy.

May your lives always be blessed with peace.

Samson and Delilah

THE CONVERSION PROPHECY

PROLOGUE

"In the beginning God created the heavens and the earth. And the earth was without form and void, and darkness was upon the face of the deep, and the Spirit of God was moving over the face of the waters. God created light; the firmament separating the waters, dry land and seas, and plants and trees, which grew fruit with seed; the sun, moon, and stars in the firmament; air-breathing sea creatures and birds; and on the sixth day, the beasts of the earth according to their kinds. Then God said, 'Let us make man in the image of God.' He created them; male and female. On the seventh day He rested from the task of completing the heavens and the earth: So God blessed the seventh day and hallowed it, because on it God rested from all his work which he had done in creation. The land that He created was serene and of peace. And God saw that it was good."

- From the Book of Genesis

And so it began. Later man and woman replicated, creating families who then multiplied even further. As the earth became inhabited, tribes developed and formed their own beliefs about the Creator and who it was that guided them spiritually.

Over the years, decades, and centuries that followed, many wars have been fought in the name of religion trying to impose one group's will against another. These conflicts continued for thousands of years and have never been resolved. In recent times there was an epoch of international terrorism in which the will of one religious group tried to force its beliefs on the rest of the world. When that didn't succeed, they stopped their vicious ways in favor of pursuing a more peaceful but devious plan to bring the world to its knees. They have to be stopped.

CHAPTER 1

Death came swiftly and unexpectedly. It was a day in December. The date and time don't matter anymore, but it was the point when life ceases and everything stops, even time. He lay there alone, motionless and breathless. His skin was getting colder and paler by the minute. Every cell of his body was devoid of life.

It was less than twenty-four hours earlier that he'd had a complete medical exam and passed without a ripple. It has baffled medical science for years, how a person can have a complete medical work-up, be found to be in perfect health, and suddenly die that evening. There have been people who left a doctor's office with a clean bill of health only to go into cardiac arrest and fall to the ground dead before they reached their car. Was that the case with Joseph Karlin—or was there something sinister about his death?

Was it swift and painless? Most people say if they had a choice, they would want to die in their sleep peacefully. But is it peaceful? No one really knows if dying in your sleep is painless and peaceful. What does a person really feel? Is there a subconscious feeling of slipping away that only the dying can explain? Does the brain feel pain for the very first time? However, with whom can the dead communicate? For the stricken, it is far too late.

The second floor of the house was still. The only other people in the house were the domestic staff, who were preparing for the morning feast to come. You could smell the sweetness of hot muffins as they were removed from the oven. The odor of fresh brewed coffee permeated the room as the sound of frying bacon could be heard by those within earshot.

It was 6:18 A.M. In twelve minutes, his personal security aide would knock at his bedroom door to awaken him. A morning jog, a breakfast meeting with old friends, a staff meeting at his office over lunch, and an afternoon photo-op were going to occupy the day. Today, that would be impossible.

Six minutes earlier, veteran Secret Service agent Ron Moss entered the house through the garage entrance, where he had been on sentry duty since arriving for his 4:00 A.M. to 12:00 noon tour. Moss, thirty-eight years old, six feet tall, brown haired, and with steel blue eyes, had been a member of the Secret Service for twelve years. He had joined the service after completing his Bachelor's Degree in Criminal Justice from John Jay College in New York.

Extremely athletic, he worked out daily. After completing a one-hour weight training routine, he topped it off with a forty-five-minute five-mile run. He also worked out twice a week with his Sensei, to maintain his proficiency as a black belt in karate. He was married for six years, which had ended in divorce seven years earlier. The marriage did not produce any children. However, he and his former wife remained friends and occasionally had dinner together.

Moss lived alone in a two-bedroom apartment in Georgetown. He was meticulous in his manner and dress. His temperament was cheerful but resolute. He paid attention to detail and was always cognizant of his surroundings. Ron Moss had a photographic mind and remembered minor details. He was something of a loner. However, the few friends he had maintained from college called him "Computer Ron" because of his total recall, to an extent that is almost unheard of. He had remarried, and his new spouse was his job.

He proceeded through the pantry kitchen to the stairs that led to the second floor. At 6:30, a gentle knock echoed throughout the hall of the second floor as Moss tapped on the white wood paneled door, the sound reverberating off the hardwood oak floors. When there was no answer, he followed it with a second knock about twenty seconds later. When another thirty seconds passed, the caller knocked again with the knuckles of his left hand as he opened the bedroom door with his right and called out to his charge, "Good morning, sir."

Stepping into the room, he walked to the window, the plush carpet beneath his feet silencing his steps. He drew back the curtains, allowing the bright outside light to enter the room in a sudden flash. The morning sun, which was rising, illuminated the 18-by-30-foot room. It exposed the king-sized mahogany sleigh bed and two matching night stands, which each contained a faux Tiffany lamp. They were centered on the wall opposite that which held the framed glass that separated the room from the outside world. A beige love seat and wood coffee table were perpendicular to the bed. Two matching overstuffed upholstered chairs were placed opposite the love seat.

A pair of grey slacks, its belt still looped around the waistband, was lying across the arm of one chair. A white dress shirt was draped over the back of the chair, with a blue-and-white-striped tie still affixed to it through its button-down collar. A pair of black wing-tipped shoes stuffed with socks were next to the chair. They seemed to have been placed there in haste.

As Moss turned toward the bed, once again he called out loudly, "Good morning, sir." There was still no answer. It was at that moment his senses told him something was terribly wrong, as his nose inhaled the scent of stale air, like that of a dusty room that lacked ventilation.

As he turn toward the bed, he saw the pale, motionless body for the first time that morning. He was lying under the sheets with his arms at his side. The brightness shone across his face. Stepping quickly to the side of the bed, Ron attempted to rouse its occupant by gently shaking his bare arm. The flesh of his forearm was cold and clammy, like a piece of refrigerated raw meat. His face was pale, and his eyes were closed. There was an expression of pain on his face that seemed to show signs of an internal struggle.

Moss froze in his place for an instant. He placed the index and middle finger of his right hand against the chilled neck of his charge, feeling for a pulse. Nothing! His chest was not rising and falling because there was no breath. Moss then reacted out of instinct, knowing what he needed to do. Without hesitation, he hurriedly reached for the phone on the night stand, his hand bumping into a cup of tea that almost spilled the remnants of the liquid it contained, the cup tilting back, then rocking forward, coming to a rest in the saucer that held it in place.

"Naval medics. Do you have an emergency?"

"This is Agent Ron Moss. I have a code 1086 and need paramedics at this location ASAP."

"Yes, Agent Moss," the voice responded.

Moss hung up the phone and briefly thought about administering CPR. Realizing that at this time it would be fruitless, he decided against it. He had seen enough death in his career to know when and when not to try heroic lifesaving efforts. As far as he was concerned, it was hopeless. Moss felt helpless. *The poor guy has probably been dead for hours,* he thought to himself.

Moss decided to maintain radio silence. He raced down the fifteen steps to the floor below so fast that it was as though his feet never touched the stair treads. Opening the front door, he screamed out to the two suited men standing guard out front, "Paramedics are on the way! Dave, get in here!" Dave Foster, an eight-year veteran of the Service, rushed toward the door. "It doesn't look good," Moss said. "He may have been dead for hours, apparently in his sleep."

"Tell me you're joking," Foster said as he quickly slipped from his overcoat and dropped it on a nearby chair in the reception hall. He really didn't mean what he said. You don't joke about these things, and he knew it.

"Lock down the house," Moss said with authority.

"I'm on it." Foster immediately opened a secure closet and unplugged all the incoming telephone lines except one, which was attached to a secure phone in the study on the second floor. This line required a six-digit code to be entered before a call could be initiated. They did not want the staff to be able to make any outgoing calls. He then rounded up the house staff and told them that the house was in lock-down for security reasons. They had been through this before, so there was no anxiety on the part of the staff. All the other times it had been just precautionary, or a drill with no real threat. This time things were different.

The kitchen staff just went about their business preparing the morning feast for the guests who were to arrive later that morning.

Moss met the paramedics as they rushed into the house. "I only need you to confirm my findings. I am sure there is nothing you can do at this point. After that, I'm afraid I can't let you leave until the proper notifications are made."

"I understand," said Peter Hooke, the first medic who responded. The paramedics followed Moss to the master suite, where the body was at rest. Although there was no doubt that he was dead, Hooke pulled back the sheets and placed his stethoscope to listen for a heartbeat. He held it in place for what seemed an eternity. He then moved it upward to the patient's neck, looking for a carotid pulse. The results were the same. Removing it, he looked at Foster and just shook his head from side to side. The medic then shined his flashlight into the patient's eyes. The pupils were fixed. There was no reaction to the light. Once again, Peter Hooke just shook his head. He reached around and lifted the patient's shoulders as if to roll him over. It exposed the purple stains of lividity on his back, which indicated that this was not a recent demise. Taking care not to drop the patient, Hooke gently released his grip and guided the body back into its original position. "He may have been dead for hours," Hooke said.

"Thank you, guys. We just had to be sure. It just doesn't make sense," Moss said, his voice cracking a little. "The man jogs three miles every morning, plays racquet ball for two hours twice a week, skis in the winter, and plays golf when he can. He eats the right foods and takes more vitamins than anyone else I know. He had a complete medical check-up yesterday, including a stress test. How could this happen?"

"God works in strange ways," Hooke responded.

"Please wait downstairs in the sitting room. Agent Foster is there. I am sure it should not be too long. This must remain confidential until the proper notifications are made."

"We understand," the medics said in unison as they left the room.

Picking up the teacup as if to tidy up the room, Moss left the room, closing the door behind him. He then walked downstairs to the kitchen, placed the cup in the sink, turned, and proceeded back upstairs to the study.

CHAPTER 2

Ron Moss picked up the telephone handset in the study. He dialed a six-digit security code, followed by the cell phone number of Paul Day. A voice on the other end answered, "This is Paul Day. With whom am I speaking?"

"Mr. Day, this is agent Ron Moss. Are you alone?"

Paul Day, chief of staff to the president, had been the general counsel for the president's campaign and a close friend of his since their days together at the University of Miami Law School. President-elect William Prescott had asked Paul to be his chief of staff during the weeks following his election in 2024.

"Yes, agent Moss, what can I do for you?"

"I'm afraid I have bad news. It's the vice president, sir. He apparently died in his sleep." His voice was all business, something that his training had prepared him for. Even though he had been close to vice president Karlin and considered him a friend, and even though he had worked for and admired him for five years, the time to get emotional was later.

There was a pause on the other end of the line as the chief of staff tried to grasp what he had just heard. He felt his body go numb as though all his blood suddenly drained away. "My God! Are you sure?"

"Yes, sir. The naval paramedics confirmed it."

"Moss, where are you now?"

"I'm in his study on the secure phone. The house is in lock-down."

"Have you called Robert Bristol?" Bristol was his chief of staff.

"Not yet, sir. I thought it best to notify you first."

"Does anybody else know?"

"Just myself, one other agent, and the medics. They have been instructed not to leave. Agent Foster is with them making sure they don't communicate with anyone until I have made the proper notifications."

"I'll call you right back! Don't leave and don't speak to anyone!"

"Yes, sir. I'll be right here."

Day knocked on the double French doors to the president's private study in the residential section of the White House. He pushed them open without waiting for a response. President William Prescott was just completing a morning telephone call. He was seated at his desk, still in his bathrobe. Quickly surveying the room to establish that they were alone, Day glanced at the grandfather clock that was standing in the corner. It read 7:20. "Mr. President, Joe Karlin is dead, sir," he said without hesitation.

"What? How? When? My God! He just got a clean bill of health!"

"I don't have the details, sir. All I know is that when Agent Moss went to wake him for his morning jog, he found him in bed. He obviously died in his sleep."

"Does Bristol know?"

"Not yet, sir. I was about to call him."

"What about his wife and family?" he asked as he slumped into the chair behind his desk, his body going limp from shock.

"Anne is in Connecticut visiting their daughter and grandchild. We will be notifying them immediately."

"Inform Bob Bristol and tell him to keep it to himself until he hears from us. I don't want this leaked until we know more." Robert Bristol was the vice president's chief of staff, who had been at his side since he was sworn in five years earlier. A man of extremely high integrity, he had been Joseph Karlin's confidant. "Then contact my cabinet and the house leaders. Tell them to get here immediately. Get Mona. We need to call a press conference, and I need to address the nation. I'll be in my office. Paul, not a word to anyone until all notifications are properly made. I mean *no one!*"

"Yes, sir."

As the chief of staff left the study, the president removed a Bible from his desk drawer. A spiritual man, he turned to the 23rd Psalm and recited it silently to himself, then asked God for strength and guidance.

After hurriedly showering, he dressed and made his way to the Oval Office. It took him no more than twenty minutes to get ready. When he arrived, Paul Day was already there, waiting for him.

"Mona is on her way down. I told her to meet me here. She should be here in a minute. Bob Bristol is arranging for the family notification and their return to the capitol." The sounds of his last words were still in the air when the press secretary entered the Oval Office through the open door.

Mona Tieger, press secretary, was the seventh female presidential press secretary in the history of the White House. She was a tall, slender woman with long red hair. At forty-eight years of age, she had total confidence in herself and had complete control of the White House press corps.

A graduate of the School of Journalism at the University of Missouri, she had formerly been a news anchor on two major networks. She knew the inner workings of the press from every angle. She was a party loyalist and someone the press thought highly of. Hardworking, she could be found at her desk by 6:30 every morning.

"Good morning, Mr. President," she said as she entered the room.

"Mona, please close the door and have a seat."

As Mona sank into the blue sofa cushions, the president's jarring words assaulted her: "Sometime last night, Vice President Karlin died in his sleep."

"Oh, my God! What happened?" She began to shake, and her lips quivered as she spoke. Other than her immediate boss, President William Prescott, Joseph Karlin was the man she admired most. She was in complete shock.

"We don't have all the details yet. However, as of now, there are fewer than a handful of people who know. His residence is in lock-down. No one is allowed in or out until his family is notified. Bob Bristol is taking care of that as we speak. The only communication we have is through his secure phone with Agent Moss. The cabinet is on their way in; so are the Speaker and both House leaders. We need to call a press conference as soon as possible, but not until his family is notified. I will address the nation first. Round up the press corps and have them stand by."

"Yes, Mr. President," she answered as she reached for a tissue and wiped the tears from her eyes. She was a professional and regained her composure immediately. Mona knew her place and knew the time for grieving was later.

Paul Day's cell phone rang. He looked at the Caller ID and answered it. "Yes, Robert." There was a pause as the president listened to Paul's side of the conversation. "I see. Thank you."

"That was Bristol. He spoke to the family priest and asked him to notify the family."

"Good. I don't envy him. It is not a task anyone would want to engage in," he said with compassion in his voice. "Paul, have my secretary cancel all my appointments for today."

"Consider it done."

Paul Day returned to his office and called Ron Moss at the vice president's residence.

"Agent Moss, we are notifying the vice president's family at this very moment. As soon as we have confirmation, I will let you know. The chief White House medical officer, Dr. Baum, is on his way over to your location. He should arrive within the next thirty minutes. He will make all the necessary arrangements for the vice president. He paused and then said, "Ron?"

"Yes, sir?"

"I know how close you were to the vice president. This must be hard for you. I know how proud he would be of you if he knew how admirable your actions were in this time of need. God bless you."

"Thank you, sir," he said, his voice choking a little.

CHAPTER 3

Anne Tavis had grown up in Rye Brook, New York, as an only child. Although her father had been a prominent attorney, he had never run for public office despite having dabbled in local politics. Her mother had been a medical doctor. A female general practitioner was uncommon in the early 1960s. For most of Anne's younger years, she was cared for by a live-in nanny. As Anne grew older, she attended private schools and eventually went on to Brandeis University where, to her mother's disappointment, she studied Political Science. It seemed as though there was going to be another lawyer in the family, not another doctor.

After Brandeis, where she graduated summa cum laude, Anne completed her legal studies at Yale University in New Haven, Connecticut. It was there that she met the handsome and bright Joseph Karlin. He had spoken to the graduates as a representative of the Yale Alumni Association. His remarks impressed her. After the ceremony she sought him out to tell him how dynamic he was. Two nights later, they had dinner. Fourteen months later, they were married at an elaborate reception at the Westchester Country Club in Rye, New York. She was now Mrs. Anne Tavis Karlin, the wife of Joseph Karlin, a democrat and law secretary to the Administrative Judge of the Supreme Court of Connecticut.

Anne did not enter into private practice; she accepted a position at Yale, teaching Constitutional Law. Three years later Anne gave birth to a healthy girl, their only child. They named her Margaret Grace, after Ann's maternal grandmother, whom she never knew. When Margaret Grace was in her third year of high school, Joseph found himself in a race for Congress in his district. He won by a landslide. His re-election two years later was a runaway. In his last election, he ran unopposed. After seven terms of representing his district, Joe Karlin was asked by William Prescott, Republican candidate for president, to be his running mate. It was the first time candidates from opposing parties had been on the same ticket. The country needed to be healed, and the only way it was going to happen was with a fusion ticket. Their combined popularity helped to sweep them into office. He had been nearing the end of the first year of his second term as vice president when he his life was tragically taken from him at the age of sixty-three.

Anne was in the kitchen feeding her granddaughter breakfast. She was not scheduled to return to Washington until 1:00 P.M. Margaret Grace, who had become a plastic surgeon, was sitting opposite her, drinking a cup of coffee. Margaret's husband, Dr. Jeffery Barnes, a thoracic surgeon, was already at work at Westchester Medical Center in Valhalla, New York, where he was performing a triple bypass on a fifty-five-year-old male patient. Theresa, their live-in housekeeper and nanny, was at the sink rinsing some dishes.

"You know, Mom, maybe you should let me take care of those bags under your eyes and tighten up your face a little."

"I'm not ready for your artistic abilities on the human body just yet. Your father has no complaints and neither should you."

"There's no rush, Mom. You can wait until Dad runs for president. This way, you will look younger when you campaign." They both chuckled. Even though the possibility of her husband running for president had been discussed before, it was too early to make any definitive decisions yet.

"I do not want to discuss it right now. Maybe someday in the future. There are more important things on my plate right now."

Their conversation was abruptly interrupted as Secret Service agent Bob Daly suddenly appeared in the doorway. Standing behind him was Father Vincent Cagninni, the family's parish priest since they had lived in

Cos Cob, Connecticut. The son of second generation Italian immigrants, the sixty-eight-year-old priest was about five-feet-seven inches tall. His olive complexion was framed by his dark brown hair, which was sprinkled with grey. He was dressed in the cloth of his church. His usual smile was replaced by sadness in his brown eyes.

Noticing Father Cagninni, Anne said, "Vincent, how nice to see you. I am so glad you stopped by." She rose from her chair and walked to the doorway, where agent Daly and Father Cagninni were standing. Anne noticed that his face was somber. Then she noticed his eyes.

"Anne, can I have a word with you, please?"

The priest reached for her hand and guided her toward the green plush sofa in the family room adjoining the kitchen. As she sat down, she suddenly realized that something was terribly wrong. She became frightened at the look on both of their faces. Father Cagninni sat next to her and gently held her hands in his.

Daly excused himself, stepped into the kitchen, and exited through the rear door onto the patio. A light December snow was crunching beneath his feet as he spoke into the microphone clipped to the inside cuff of his jacket sleeve. His eyes gazed skyward as two other agents were scratching a circle in the half-inch of snow that had fallen the night before. They were creating a target in the acre-sized yard for a helicopter to land that would take the family to Westchester County airport, where they would meet Air Force Two for the return to the Capitol.

"You're frightening me, Vincent. Is something wrong?"

"Anne, it's Joseph. The good Lord has called for him. He passed away suddenly in his sleep last night."

A loud bellowing scream echoed throughout the house. "Noooo! It can't be true!"

Margaret came running into the room to find her mother shaking and crying uncontrollably as Father Cagninni held her in his arms. "Mom, what's wrong?" she shouted.

"It's your father, Margaret," she cried out loudly, her voice cracking and barely coherent.

"He apparently had a fatal heart attack in his sleep last night," Father Cagninni said, finishing her statement.

"Oh, my God, no!" she shouted as she ran to her mother and slumped onto the sofa next to her. Holding each other tightly, the two women cried uncontrollably. Tears welled up in Father Cagninni's eyes as well. He had married Jeffery and Margaret, had christened their daughter, and had been the family's spiritual leader for the past 15 years. He had communicated dreadful news many times before. However, this was different. Joseph Karlin, a gentle, compassionate, deeply religious man had been on a path to becoming the most powerful person in the free world. Now that would never be.

CHAPTER 4

As the president's cabinet gathered in the cabinet room of the White House, they speculated among themselves as to why this sudden meeting. They knew it was not any terrorist attacks. There had not been any in the world since the new peace agreement had been signed four years before, thanks to the efforts of the secretary of state, a position that was held by Robert Amanti, a former senator from Georgia. There wasn't any buzz in their offices from the press, and nothing of any consequence on the morning news. Maybe the president just wanted to present a new idea to them. But then why the sudden urgency? They milled around the room, some drinking coffee or snacking on muffins from the platter of breakfast breads that were served at morning meetings. They were speculating among themselves but didn't have any answers.

"Mr. President, the notifications have been made," Chief of Staff Day said as he entered the Oval Office. "It's time to meet with the cabinet, sir."

As Paul Day and the president were walking toward the cabinet room, Secretary Tieger was double-timing it from behind. She wanted to intercept them before they entered the room. "Mr. President," she called out.

"Yes, Mona?" He stopped and turned to face her.

"Mr. President, the press will be in the briefing room at 10:45. I have already cleared the networks for you to go on the air at that time from the Oval Office. After you report to the nation, I will meet with the press and bring them up to date on whatever details we have. Is there anything new I should know?"

"No. Right now our information is limited to what we already know, and that isn't much."

At the vice president's residence, Dr. Seth Baum, chief White House physician, was examining the body of Joseph Karlin. With him in the bedroom were FBI director Robert Berry and Gene Coates, director of the NSA.

"Everything looks natural," the fifty-two-year-old physician said. "Of course, I definitely want a pathological exam to rule out everything. In reality, though, everything on the surface says natural causes. What a terrible shame and a waste for a great man to have his life cut short before he fulfilled his potential."

President Prescott entered the cabinet room. Everyone stood up in respect. Secretary Tieger stood off to the side of the conference table with Paul Day. William Prescott stood behind his chair at the center of the long conference table. His left hand was resting on the top of the large leather chair. His right hand, which held his Bible, was at his side. He did not take his seat first, which was unusual. He wanted to address those present from a standing position. "Good morning, ladies and gentlemen. Please be seated." He was soft spoken, with a sadness in his voice. As he glanced around the table at those present, it was obvious that there was one empty seat. He was visibly shaken. He tried to hide his anxiety, but he wore it on his sleeve. It appeared that all the cabinet members suddenly realized this was not going to be good news.

The president continued, without pausing between sentences. "It is with a heavy heart that I must inform you that sometime during the night Vice President Joseph Karlin apparently suffered a heart attack and has passed away. He was found by Agent Moss, who went to wake him for his daily jog."

The room fell silent, so silent that if a fly had walked across the table you could have heard its footsteps. A buzz and chatter in the room followed immediately as those assembled expressed their disbelief. "My God, we played racquetball on Monday, and he never looked better," exclaimed the secretary of the Interior.

"I am shocked! He had a complete physical just yesterday," echoed the Treasury secretary. "I had dinner with him last night. He was jovial and his usual self, didn't complain about a thing."

The comments continued for a few minutes as most eyes wandered toward the empty seat that was usually occupied by the vice president.

"Ladies and gentlemen, please join me as we pray for his soul and for his family." The president opened his Bible as the group stood with their heads bowed. For the second time that morning, William Prescott recited the 23rd Psalm.

At the same time the President was notifying the cabinet, the wings of Air Force Two, carrying Anne Karlin, Margaret Grace, and Father Cagninni, were cutting through the light snow that was falling on the runways of Westchester County Airport, for the ninety-minute flight back to Langley Airfield. Dr. Jeffery Barnes would be joining them later when he was finished with his surgical duties. A private plane was standing by to ferry him to Washington.

Joseph Karlin was being transported to Walter Reed Medical Center Mortuary, where the chief resident pathologist, under the watchful eyes of Dr. Baum, would perform the autopsy. The examination would not begin until the vice president's family had had a chance to say goodbye in a dignified manner.

The cabinet meeting was winding down at 10:18 A.M. as the president answered as many of the questions as he had answers for. The one subject that was not broached was that of choosing a successor. It was too early to even think about it, even though some in the room had their own short list in their minds. Speculation would be up to the press to bandy about, as usual.

"Ladies and gentlemen, it is time for me to address the nation. I only ask that you remain with me in the Oval Office until after I inform the

American people. I would appreciate it if your departments were not informed until the nation knows." He wanted the nation to hear the news from him, not some department underling who would leak it to the press surreptitiously.

As the president prepared to leave the room, the assembled members rose at the same time. Echoes of "Yes, Mr. President," were heard in response to his last request. As he turned to leave, the president once more said aloud, "May God bless Joseph Karlin and his beloved family, and may God bless America."

At 10:45 A.M. all the major networks and major cable news networks transmitted a similar message: "We interrupt this program to take you to the White House, where the president is about to address the nation."

The brief address took the nation by surprise. It lasted less than four minutes. When it was over, the president dismissed his cabinet.

Mona Tieger was in the press briefing room where the members of the White House press corps were viewing the president's remarks along with the press secretary.

As expected, as soon as the president finished his remarks, the questions from the media were flying through the air like confetti in Times Square on New Year's Eve. The where, what, who, and how questions were answered with short statements that contained any information the press secretary had. Questions pertaining to a replacement or short list were immediately and sternly met with, "No thoughts have been expressed with any regard to who will replace Vice President Karlin, and I will not address any further questions pertaining to the subject."

The meeting lasted about fifteen minutes. It ended with her saying, "the vice president's family will be making the necessary arrangements. When we know the details, you will be briefed. Thank you and good day." She stepped down from the podium and exited the room. *My God, the man's body is still warm, and these vultures want to pick his bones,* Mona thought to herself.

As with the death of any governmental official, all foreign embassies in the host country are informed of the death of an elected official with a formal notification. So too, this was the case in Washington. The ambassador or his aide will then notify their country's prime minister or president of the passing.

The ambassador from the consulate of the Islamic Union called his president and pronounced the vice president's passing with just three short words: "It has begun."

CHAPTER 5

Anne Karlin and Margaret Grace were leaving Walter Reed Hospital, where they had just viewed the vice president and completed the necessary formal and legal identification. Anne was dressed in black wool slacks, and black calf-length suede boots. A beige waist-length leather jacket covered her grey turtleneck sweater. Her hair was thrown back in a ponytail and her face carried little makeup. Anne's cheeks showed the streaky black stains of her tears mixed with the mascara she had applied earlier that morning. They were standing in a white marble corridor that had an overpowering smell of Lysol disinfectant.

Secret Service agents were positioned at both ends of the hallway to give them privacy as well as protection. Father Cagninni accompanied them.

Agent Ron Moss was also there; he had stayed with the vice president's body from the time it left his residence. Facing Anne Karlin, he held her hands in his and expressed how sorry he was. She said, "Thank you, Ron. You have been more than our security; you have been a dear friend to both of us."

As they were exiting the hospital, the president and First Lady Lillian Prescott met them. William Prescott was the first to approach Anne. He embraced her and whispered in her ear, "Anne, I can only believe that the good Lord has more important work for Joseph to tend to. He is a wonderful husband, father, grandfather, father-in-law, statesman, and friend. We are all going to miss him very much." He consciously spoke of Joseph Karlin in the present tense.

"Thank you, William. I know how close you were to him," she said through her tears. William Prescott was wiping tears from his eyes as Lillian Prescott, the first lady, stepped in to hug Anne.

The president turned to Margaret Grace and hugged her. The four of them stood in a tight embrace as Father Cagninni led them in a short prayer. "May you keep Joseph in your embrace, Lord, and protect him in heaven and his family on earth. Amen."

As they continued down the hall to their respective limousines, the curtain to the viewing room was closing. The pathologist was about to attend to the body so it could quickly be released to lie in state in the Capitol Rotunda as with all past presidents and vice presidents.

One day after the public viewing of the flag-draped silver casket, in the Capitol Rotunda, the late vice president, Joseph Karlin, was moved to Yale University's Sprague Memorial Hall for a televised funeral service. It was attended by every member of the Senate, House of Representatives, and cabinet, as well as fourteen foreign heads of state.

Father Cagninni officiated at the service. It was concluded with a memorial speech delivered by President Prescott. Vice President Karlin was then moved to his final resting place on the side of a small hill, in the cemetery behind Father Cagninni's parish church. There was a brief graveside service attended by the immediate family, the First Family, a select few cabinet members, and some close family friends and relatives.

Two weeks later the pathologist's report on Joseph Karlin was finalized and filed away, with just four short words: "Death by natural causes." There was no evidence of anything that might have contributed to his death. Every test imaginable showed that his heart just quit without any underlying cause. He simply ran out of time.

CHAPTER 6

Within days of the vice president's funeral, things quickly returned to normal in Washington and the rest of the country. The only pressing task in the Oval Office was to choose a successor to Joseph Karlin. Although the press had been speculating since the announcement of the death of the vice president, there was no indication from the White House as to who was on a short list. President Prescott had his own choice in mind, and it seemed that his short list contained only one name: Secretary of State Robert Amanti.

When nominated and confirmed at age fifty, Robert Amanti had been the youngest sitting cabinet member. He was appointed and confirmed unanimously by the Senate in the second year of the previous administration's second term in office. President Prescott asked him to stay on as secretary of state; a position he now holds longer than any previous cabinet member. His job performance had been exemplary. He was held in the highest regard by the leaders of nations throughout the world. Amanti and his undersecretary were principally responsible for the dialogues that had taken place that had led to the unbelievable peace and prosperity in the world over the last few years. There was no doubt in the president's mind that he would be confirmed quickly.

Robert was born and raised in Atlanta, Georgia as an only child. His father had been a prominent attorney, and his mother had taught elementary school until he was born. He excelled in his studies and graduated at the top of his class. It was not a surprise when he applied for and was accepted to Harvard University.

After receiving his Bachelor's degree in Political Science, Robert continued at Harvard Law School. It was there, as a second year student, that he met and befriended Barry Melat. Barry was a Moslem-American, who was born in the U.S. They became close friends. Although the same age, Barry was a year behind in school because he had taken a year off after receiving his undergraduate degree to travel abroad.

When he graduated and received his Juris Doctorate, Robert accepted a position with Glaser, Zimmerman, and Roth a large law firm in Atlanta.

Barry Melat interned at Robert's firm his last summer before graduation. When he received his Juris Doctorate, he was offered a position in the same firm through Robert's recommendation. Over the years, they worked on numerous cases together.

Two years after he joined the firm, Robert married Carolyn Massi, a young woman he had met and dated for two years. They were married at a friend's home in an intimate ceremony. Barry Melat stood as Robert's best man. The bride, who became Mrs. Carolyn Amanti, had no idea what her life would be like in the years to come.

Robert was made partner within five years.

In his ninth year with the firm, Robert decided to enter politics. He campaigned for and was elected to represent his district in the U.S. Congress. After two congressional terms, he ran for and was elected as U.S. senator from the state of Georgia.

His work on the Foreign Relations Committee earned him the respect of both parties. When he was nominated and confirmed as secretary of state, in the middle of his second senatorial term of office, he asked Barry Melat to become his undersecretary.

Together they made over twenty trips to the Middle East. Both as senator and as secretary, Robert was responsible for the peaceful relations that took place between the Arab nations and the rest of the world. The United States, under the guidance of President Prescott and with the abundant help of the secretary, regained its place as the world's leading nation. And just a year before the vice president's untimely passing, Robert Amanti had been awarded the Nobel Prize for Peace.

There was little doubt who the president's choice for second-in-command would be. When he announced it to the Senate, there was hardly a ripple. Robert Amanti was confirmed in a simple up and down vote.

Agent Ron Moss had a choice of being reassigned; however, not wanting to change personnel who were already in place, the new vice president asked Moss to stay on in his position.

"I heard how close you were with Vice President Karlin. I hope that we can develop the same rapport, Ron."

"I don't see why not, Mr. Vice President." Agent Ron Moss took his place beside his new assignment.

Eleven days after the announcement, Robert Amanti was sworn in as vice president of the United States. The only task now was to fill the cabinet vacancy that was left as a result of the appointment of the new vice president.

At the suggestion of the new vice president, President Prescott nominated Undersecretary Barry Melat. It was well known that Melat, a Moslem-American, was a natural born citizen of the U.S. under the fourteenth amendment, since his mother had given birth to him while his parents were working in the United States.

At the age of nineteen, Barry had suddenly found himself orphaned. His parents were in a horrendous traffic accident while vacationing in California. Their car burst into flames after hurling off a cliff on the Pacific Coast Highway.

Barry Melat had been the undersecretary and right-hand man of the man who was now vice president. His boss attributed the peace that was now present in the world to Melat's work on establishing the dialogue that had been needed in the Middle East. There were some early rumblings in the press that as a young man, he had attended a madrassa while living in Indonesia for a year. However, those allegations could not be corroborated.

"Mr. President, I believe he is a sound choice and would continue in the manner with which we have conducted the affairs of the State Department. I am certain he would not disappoint you or the nation, sir."

"What about the Senate? Do you think we will have any trouble with his confirmation?"

"I doubt it. Religious beliefs have been cohesive in America. I doubt the Senate will have any objection because he is a Moslem. Besides, with the world being the way it is today, he would probably have a better chance of keeping the peace than anyone. The people will not care if a Moslem is part of our cabinet. Besides, his character is beyond reproach. He is an American first and a Moslem second. He is an outstanding member of his community, an outstanding member of this administration, and a great jurist. I have known him since we were at Harvard together. We were inseparable. We went on to Harvard Law together. I would trust him with my life. And remember, it is the State Department that was responsible for the new treaties between us, the European and Islamic Unions, and the Pacific Rim Nations."

"Then the undersecretary it will be," the president said.

After a short Senate hearing and an up-and-down vote, Barry Melat was sworn in as the new secretary of state.

CHAPTER 7

A group of young students walked down an old cobblestone street that led to the great mosque that sat in the center of the village. Its great golden dome, surrounded by five minarets, stood as the highest structure in this small metropolis. One student seemed to stand out from the rest. His complexion was not that of the typical Moslem child who attended the school. His skin was paler, and his demeanor was different. His straight brown hair seemed to frame his face, which held a pair of bright blue eyes that reflected his surroundings. He was an American. Although he was an American citizen, born in the U.S. of American parents, his religious studies were in the mosque.

His father, Alan, was a third generation American Moslem. His mother, Sylvia, was Jewish by birth. Her parents were Americans of German Jewish heritage, which may have accounted for the boy's light complexion and blue eyes. Although their household was secular because of their different religious backgrounds, they chose to have their son learn of all religious faiths. What better place to learn about Islam than right here in Indonesia? His academic studies were conducted at the American school all expatriates attended. He was an exceptionally gifted child and was ahead in his studies. He had a thirst for knowledge. He loved to read.

They had moved here after Alan, an engineer, accepted a position as project director for the Ameri-Pro Corporation. He was now at the end of his eleventh year of a ten-year assignment, and it did not look as if they would be returning to the States any time soon. His project was to construct a new reservoir and hydroelectric dam to produce potable water and electricity for the region.

Six months after they had arrived, Sylvia, gave birth to a healthy seven-pound-two-ounce boy. Alan and she had returned to Atlanta so that their son would be born in the United States and have full rights as a citizen. They named him Michael Hussein Haman. His middle name was derived from that of his paternal great-grandfather, Hussein Haman, whom he would never know except in family photos.

As the group entered the mosque, they scattered in separate directions, only to meet up in a common classroom.

Michael was met by another Moslem-American, who was his teacher. His name was Arbry Tamel, thirty-two years old, about five feet eleven inches tall, 185 pounds, with black hair, a full beard, and mustache. A devout Moslem, Arbry was on assignment from a mosque in America, sent to learn the duties of a muezzin, an imam's assistant. He had taken Michael under his wing and seemed to give him special attention. They walked together through the large, cavernous mosque, where every whisper echoed throughout as the smallest sound bounced off the ancient marble walls.

Each was carrying his own Qur'an. Hand-woven prayer rugs were scattered over the floor. They entered a room at the far end of the mosque where their imam, Mhamet Salem, greeted them. Because he had lived there since birth, Michael was bilingual. He spoke both English and Bahasa, the primary language spoken in Indonesia.

"It is time for you to practice your prayers, boys."

"Yes, Imam," the group responded in Bahasa. As they knelt on their prayer rugs, Imam Salem left the room through a side door that led outside. He was greeted by a man known as Ahmed Samu, the imperial imam of the region. Samu was forty-five-years-old, six feet tall, with black hair and deep set dark eyes. He was dressed in a white thobe, a long, one-piece, loose-fitting, white cotton garment that resembled a long shirt. It completely covered his arms and continued down to his ankles. His feet were adorned in brown sandals. His thobe was covered by a gold-colored Bisht, which indicated he was a religious leader. The two men left and walked slowly side by side in the garden that was adjacent to the mosque. They spoke in Bahasa. "How are they doing?" Samu asked.

"Very well. I believe the younger American will grow to be smarter than the other. However, the older one, Arbry, who I believe is just as smart, is really here to learn of our plans. He is true to our faith. Our plans are to help him move into the political arena in America; after which he will take on the role he has been chosen for. He will be here for only a short time. The boy is much too young. We cannot wait that long. Our people are grooming Arbry as our future leader and know he will be up to the task."

"So you believe he will be ready to carry out our plans years from now?"

"Yes! I have no doubt. He is a true believer and is ready to complete his mission. I know he will not fail us. My only regret is that it may take another ten years to start the process and another ten to complete it. With my failing health I may not be here to see it through to its execution, but I know there will be others who will follow me to assure the twelfth imam returns."

"The other one you speak of, the younger one named Michael—my sources tell me he was born in the United States. I am certain we can continue his education in America. When will you begin his training?"

"It has already begun. The seeds are being sown as we speak. Arbry knows his mission; he has begun to groom his pupil. We just have to assure the boy returns to America so we can continue his education there. We can complete it through the society. His father has disgraced our faith by marrying an outsider. Worse than that, she is a Jew. He will be dealt with."

"How so?"

"It is being planned. Arbry and our people are taking care of the details as we speak."

"Good, Salem. I must leave now. May Allah be with you."

"Peace be with you, my brother."

The boys were finishing their prayers as the imam re-entered the room. "Boys, I want to commend you on your studies. You are all very bright. You may go and play soccer if you wish."

As the students left for a grassless patch of soil at the rear of the mosque, Michael and Arbry were asked to stay behind.

"Michael, you are the smartest one in your class. I am going to suggest to your parents that you attend different classes that will give you a better appreciation of your education."

Michael seemed excited that he was being singled out for special classes. Two weeks later, during the American school summer recess, both Michael and Arbry were sent to Jakarta for eighteen days, where they attended a madrassa. It was the start of their education in Wahhabism. Arbry was there more to keep an eye on Michael and to chaperone him than to learn for himself. He was well educated in the task ahead and knew his place within his Islamic beliefs.

Michael's days were filled with intense study. The class, which consisted of fourteen students, was allowed only one hour of recreation each day. It was more akin to brainwashing than studying. The one message that was repeated to them consistently was that the prophet of Islam, Mohammed, who said, "I was ordered to fight the people of the world until they believe in Allah and his messenger." The other edict that was constantly emphasized to them was that all Jews and Christians were the devil, and they must be converted or destroyed in order for there to be true peace in the world.

Michael was confused, knowing his mother was Jewish. He had never known her to be anything but loving and caring. He believed she was the exception because she didn't practice her religion.

Michael was passionate about his studies. His mind was a sponge that kept soaking up more, and he wanted more. On their last day, their imam said that from then on they would all be known as Wahhabi. "Your role will be to spread Islamic law to the rest of the world. Only then will there be peace on earth." They were told that they could not speak of what they had learned; however, their lessons would continue secretly when they returned home. They were also told that for keeping this secret, they would be greatly rewarded one day. From that day forward, they would also be known as Mujahidin, unifiers of Islamic practices.

When Michael returned home and resumed his studies at the mosque, he was surprised that Arbry was absent. He was told by the imam that Arbry had moved back to America and that he would probably never see him again. Michael was extremely sad at that.

As the days passed, his studying took his mind off his friend. He was immersed in his education. The more work he was given, the more he absorbed. His brain was becoming a hard drive with never-ending memory. Not only was he book smart, he was becoming faithful to his teachings. His passion and thirst for more was immense. Was it becoming his faith or his destiny?

About two months later, Michael arrived home from school to find two of his father's co-workers waiting for him. His mother was seated at the kitchen table, crying uncontrollably. As soon as she saw him enter the room, she ran and grabbed him. Holding him tight, she began to cry louder.

"Momma, what's wrong?" he asked with fear in his heart.

"Michael, it's your father—he is dead! He was killed when a large steel beam fell on him at work!" Michael started to cry, his body shaking uncontrollably. He held his mother firmly for about a minute. Suddenly he regained his composure and released his grip on his mother. He turned and ran into his room, then closed and locked the door behind him.

Reaching under his bed, he retrieved his prayer rug. Unrolling it, he knelt down, faced Mecca, and prayed the Qur'an with tears streaming down his cheeks.

One week later, Sylvia Haman and her son Michael returned to the United States. They moved in temporarily with her sister's family in a suburb of Atlanta. Sylvia was left a very rich widow, when Alan's estate and life insurance payments were finalized four months later. She collected over $3,000,000, more than enough to purchase a modest house and provide for Michael the best she could.

CHAPTER 8

There were eight pharmaceutical companies in Iran. Two of these plants were so busy that they worked two additional nightly shifts in order to complete their production schedules. The majority of the drugs they produced were shipped throughout the world.

The cargo ship Sun Moon left the port of Amirabad in Iran after it had stopped on its way from Ankara, Turkey to load five containers of pharmaceuticals that were consolidated from two of the busiest drug manufacturers in Tehran. The ship's first port of call was Catia la Mar, in Venezuela.

When the ship reached its destination, it was met at the pier by a Venezuelan customs officer, who was there to inspect its cargo as it was being offloaded. He was morbidly obese. His stomach hung over his belt. He was wearing khaki pants with a matching shirt that was straining at its buttons, trying to restrain his flesh from tearing through. His badly stained uniform was topped off with a military-style cap, which revealed perspiration stains that may have been there for months. He wore black military boots, which needed a polishing. A brass badge, pinned to his shirt, simply read CUSTOMS AGENT. His face was rough, and it appeared that he hadn't shaved in days.

A man, obviously of Middle Eastern decent, dressed in a grey suit and white shirt with no tie approached the customs officer. "Good day, Juan Carlos." The man addressed the agent as though he was not a stranger to him.

"Buenas tardes, Señor Mohamed. Are you expecting a shipment today?"

"Yes! Five containers of pharmaceuticals arriving from Tehran on the Sun Moon."

The agent handed a clipboard to Mohamed and said, "Check off which containers are yours, and I will see if I can expedite them for you. I know your medical facilities need these drugs soon."

Mohamed checked off the numbers of the five containers. When he handed the list back to Juan Carlos, there was a half-inch-thick envelope hidden on the bottom of the clipboard, which the customs agent covertly placed in his pocket after looking around to see if anyone was watching.

A group of dockworkers led by Mohamed, who supervised the receipt of the containers and checked their lock seals, loaded the containers onto three flatbed trucks. After the containers reached their destination, they were unloaded at a distribution warehouse. When the containers were emptied, there were only four whose contents were to be inventoried.

The remaining one, on a truck by itself, took a different route. It was delivered to a ranch fifty kilometers north of the city to be unloaded. Mohamed followed in a white Jeep Cherokee. The container was filled with 10 tons of pure cocaine and heroin. Did the customs agent know, or was it that he didn't want to know when he cleared the shipment?

At the ranch, Mohamed was met by Jose Camacho, the leader of the largest drug cartel in South America. He was about six feet tall, with a well-tanned complexion, brown eyes, and jet black straight hair, which was combed back into a pony tail. He was wearing a white suit and western-style black boots. He was met with a hearty hug and handshake. "Welcome, my friend. It is good to see you again so soon," Camacho said.

"It is always good to see you too. How is production going?"

"Very well. I am glad you could deliver our product sooner than expected. Things are going so well I was afraid of running out of inventory."

"We won't let that happen. When can we expect our finished product?"

"I am certain we can turn it around within two weeks."

"That is more than acceptable. My people are getting anxious."

"That is understandable. Let us get started on this shipment and keep everybody happy."

"Well said, my friend. As soon as you complete this shipment we will wire your payment as usual."

"I am not worried, we have worked too hard and long together for me to be worried about a few dollars."

After the container was emptied, it was reloaded on the truck to be returned to the pier and recycled.

The drugs were diluted, repackaged, and smuggled worldwide. They were then distributed and sold to drug addicts through street dealers all over the world. The value of this shipment would total close to $500 million. The money from these transactions would be pooled and held in various banks and financial institutions around the world.

This scenario would be repeated about four times a year for the next twelve years. Jose Camacho would not be the recipient of these funds, but he would be paid extremely handsomely for his work—well enough to afford a 110-foot yacht, a 530-acre cattle ranch, to be used as a smokescreen for his operation, a stable of women, and an investment portfolio that would total over $300 million.

The total deposits of the illicit funds over this period would total nearly twenty-four billion dollars. Through discreet controls, these funds would find their way into legitimate financial holdings, including real estate, minerals, and bank paper.

CHAPTER 9

It was 9:15 A.M. on June 10, 1996. Thirty-two-year old stockbroker Sarah Dansk was in her office at Prudential Securities in Ridgewood, New Jersey. She was daydreaming about her upcoming vacation while waiting for the markets to open, when her assistant entered her office. "There is a Mr. Ron Gilbert here to see you."

"Who is Mr. Gilbert?" Sarah asked.

"I don't know. He asked for you by name and said it was an investment matter."

"Show him in."

Sarah was a graduate of Pace University in New York. She held a Bachelor's Degree in Business and was completing her MBA on weekends in Long Island University's executive immersion program. She was married and childless. Her husband, Bradley, was the vice president of Finance for a regional bank. They lived in a modest four-bedroom colonial in Nyack, N.Y. Sarah drove a red BMW 328I to work every day, which was about twenty-three miles from her home. As she sat at her desk awaiting her visitor, she had no idea how her life was about to change financially.

Sarah rose from her desk and extended her hand to the man who had just entered her office. He was very handsome, in his late thirties, about six feet tall, with jet-black straight hair and dark eyes. He was well tanned, wearing a navy blue double-breasted sports jacket and gray slacks. A white shirt, red tie, and black loafers adorned the rest of his body. They shook hands.

"How can I help you, Mr. Gilbert?"

"I want to open a brokerage account with your firm, and I would like you to be the person responsible for my transactions. You have come highly recommended. An acquaintance of mine said you are the best at what you do," he said as he seated himself in one of the two upholstered chairs in front of Sarah's desk.

"Who would that be?" Sarah asked.

"Actually, I don't remember his name. I met him at a party over the weekend. We were talking about investments. When I told him I was looking for an investment counselor, he said you were the best and gave me your card. I just came into a large inheritance, and I need somewhere to deposit my money. So here I am."

Sarah smiled, wondering who the mystery reference could be. "I am sure I can help you. How large an inheritance are we talking about?"

"Well, before I disclose it to you, I need to be perfectly honest with you: Any disclosure about my finances must remain completely confidential."

"There are confidentiality rules, Mr. Gilbert, You have my word."

"My father passed away last month. He left me his entire estate, which is about $270,000,000. Most of it was in banks in Europe, which I have just completed consolidating. I have no other living relatives. My initial deposit with your firm would be $200,000,000."

Sarah had all she could do to keep her jaw from hitting the floor. She felt as though her blood was draining from her face and swore her heart had just skipped a couple of beats. It was a good thing Ron Gilbert couldn't see under her desk because her legs were starting to shake uncontrollably. "You did say $200,000,000, Mr. Gilbert?" Sarah asked rhetorically, while trying to stay calm.

"Yes, and please call me Ron. I will make all decisions regarding what stocks to buy or sell. I want to purchase only Fortune 500 companies. I will not speculate. I just need you to complete the transactions for me."

Two hundred million would be the largest account her office managed, and she would be the broker of record. "I can certainly handle that for you," she said, as she reached into her desk drawer to retrieve the forms needed to open the account. *Go slow,* she said to herself. *Calm down, girl. Do this right. Don't push the forms in his face too soon.* She withdrew her empty hand from her desk drawer.

"That would be fine," he said. "Let's do it."

Once again, Sarah reached into her desk drawer, this time retrieving the forms needed to open the account. As she slid them across her desk, she asked. "Can I get you a cup of coffee or a drink?" A quick thought of *Maybe I should take my clothes off* raced through her mind, but she suppressed it quickly.

"No, thank you."

"You understand that I will need confirmation of how the funds have been accumulated. Because of SEC regulations, a deposit of that size may raise some eyebrows. I will need your personal identification, and we must make sure the funds are not from an illegal source," she said. "A deposit of that size requires our legal department to scrutinize it first. I must submit it to our compliance department."

"I certainly understand. I know there will not be any problem. All my assets were accumulated aboveboard."

"I am sure they were, but we do have our rules."

"I completely understand, and I am not insulted. I anticipated that might be a prerequisite. Therefore, I have copies of all the paperwork that will show my father's fortune was earned legitimately. Most of his holdings were in European companies in the form of stocks, bonds, and real estate. When he took ill two years ago, he converted everything to cash, except for a few parcels of real estate." He handed Sarah a folder containing the required documentation.

"Because of the size of this account, I will have to confer with my manager," Sarah said. "I am sure there will be no problem. Depending how soon our compliance department completes their work, I should have the account opened by the end of the week. I will call you as soon as I have the confirmation."

"That would be fine. As soon as that is complete, if you give me the account and routing numbers, I can have the funds transferred immediately."

Ron continued to fill out the forms while Sarah picked up the telephone, dialed her manager, and asked him to come to her office. She said, "I want to introduce you to a new client."

She calculated in her mind what her future commissions from an account this size might command and believed her blood pressure was rising off the charts thinking about the hundreds of thousands of dollars that could be coming her way. She had all she could do to not smile noticeably.

As Ron was signing the last page of the application, Gary Leo entered her office. As he came through the door, Sarah rose from her chair and said, "Gary Leo, please meet Ron Gilbert. Ron has just signed on with us to manage his portfolio."

Ron rose from his seat, and the two men shook hands. After the usual pleasantries, Gary assured Ron that he was in good hands, excused himself, and left Sarah's office. Handing the completed forms to Sarah, Ron said, "I hate to run off, but I have another appointment and don't want to be late."

Her heart was still pounding. "I understand," she said as she quickly scanned the application. "Everything seems to be in order, Mr. Gilbert. I will speak with you shortly. If there is anything else I can do for you, please call me." She handed him her business card. He took it in his left hand as he shook her hand and left.

Sarah escorted him to the elevator and said goodbye as the doors closed. Their meeting had lasted about forty-five minutes.

She hurriedly returned to her office, closed the door, sat down at her desk, and pinched herself. She had been with the firm for a little over nine years, and she had never heard of anyone walking in off the street and dropping $200,000,000 on any broker's desk. She then dialed her boss once again. "Gary, I hate to bother you, but if you have a minute, I want to speak with you."

"Sure, Sarah, I'm here."

Sarah hurried down the hall to Gary's office. She was so excited she couldn't feel her feet touching the carpeted floor as she raced the seventy feet to reach his office. "What's up?" Gary asked as she walked into his office. Closing the door behind her, she sat down. She was visibly shaking. "Are you all right?" he asked.

"I think so," she responded. "The guy I introduced you to ten minutes ago, Ron Gilbert, well h-h-h-he-he," she was stammering, "just dropped t-t-t-two hundred million on my desk."

"He what?" Gary exclaimed.

"Y-Y-Y-You h-h-heard me, two hundred million." She was having trouble catching her breath.

"Calm down, Sarah." He reached for a pitcher of water on the side of his desk and poured her a glass.

"And he wants me to handle all his transactions personally," Sarah continued after sipping some water. "He doesn't want us to set up any investment strategies for him. He just wants us to clear his transactions. He will make all decisions on what to buy or sell." She was talking out loud as if to herself, almost forgetting she was not alone. Her eyes were fixed; she spoke as if she were in a trance and had just awakened from a dream to find out she really did win the lottery.

"Wow! What a home run! Congratulations! I believe that may be one of the largest individual accounts in the firm. I know it's the largest in this office. Make sure you have all your T's crossed and I's dotted."

"Don't worry, I'm going over every piece of paper with a fine-tooth comb," she answered, as she came out of her momentary trance. "All his records are being sent to Compliance as soon as I get back to my office."

"Where did you pick him up?"

"He was referred by a client of mine."

"You certainly owe that client a big thank-you."

"It would be nice if I knew who it was. They met at a party. He doesn't remember his name. All he had was my business card."

"Wow! What a great catch. We shouldn't let this one out until the money's in the bank."

"Fine with me," Sarah countered, as she rose and left the office. Her next stop was the ladies' room.

When she returned to her office, she called her husband at work. "Brad, how does caviar, lobster, and champagne sound for dinner? It's on me."

CHAPTER 10

George Paler, a vice president at Morgan Stanley, had just completed a routine morning morale-boosting staff meeting. He was walking to his office when his secretary, Margery, met him in the hallway and said, "There is a gentleman by the name of Peter Sanders waiting in your office."

"What is it in reference to?" George inquired.

"I don't know. He said it was a personal investment matter."

"Thank you, Margery."

At fifty-two, Paler stood five-feet-eleven-inches tall, weighed about 180 pounds, and had brown hair and brown eyes. A graduate of New York University, he held both an undergraduate degree in business and an MBA. He had been married to his childhood sweetheart, Carol, for the past thirty years. Carol was an account manager with a large New York advertising agency. They had two children, a twenty-eight-year-old daughter, who held a law degree and was clerking for a State Supreme Court justice. Their twenty-five-year-old son was finishing his PhD in psychology at the University of Pennsylvania. They lived in Upper

Saddle River, New Jersey. George commuted to work every day by riding the railroad to Hoboken and ferrying the Hudson River to his financial district office. He had been with Morgan Stanley for eighteen years and had been managing this office for the past six. He had fifty-six stockbrokers working under him and a support staff of forty-two.

As George Paler re-entered his office, Peter Sanders stood up and extended his hand. He was about six feet tall, with brown hair and brown eyes, and was dressed impeccably. He was wearing a navy blue suit, a white oxford shirt, and red-and-blue-striped tie. He had long sideburns and a neatly trimmed mustache. His feet were covered with wing-tipped-style black loafers. "Mr. Paler, good morning. My name is Peter Sanders. Let's discuss the possibility of your office handling my finances," he said as the two men shook hands. His voice carried a British accent.

George Paler's office was decorated very contemporarily. His large eighty-by-forty-inch black glass desk with chrome framed legs occupied a small portion of his twenty-by-thirty-two-foot office. It was accompanied by four Lucite armchairs with black leather seat cushions, which rested on a light grey plush wall-to-wall carpet. His book-shelves were five chrome and glass étagères placed around the office walls. Their shelves contained very few books and contained mostly glass sculptures and family photos. The wall opposite his desk contained a large black leather sofa with a glass and chrome coffee table. The wall above the sofa was covered by three sixty-inch monitors, which illuminated the tickers from each of the stock markets.

"Please be seated, Mr. Sanders."

"Please call me Peter."

"Okay, if you'll call me George. How can I assist you?"

"I recently moved to New York from the U.K., and since I will be living in America, I only believe it natural that my money should follow me."

"That's a reasonable decision."

"I have a cousin in New York who believes that Morgan Stanley is one of most prestigious brokerages, and that is where my money should be."

"Please, thank your cousin for me. Is he a client of ours?"

"I am not certain. His name is Sean Seaman, a cousin on my mother's side. He gave me your name, claims he met you at a charity golf function at Winged Foot in Westchester."

"Oh sure, I think I remember him. I meet so many people, it's hard to keep up sometimes."

What a bullshit artist this guy is. He is worse than me, Peter thought. *I don't have a cousin named Sean, and I don't believe for a minute this guy ever set foot at Winged Foot.*

"I really do not need any investment advice or money management. I make my own investment decisions. I merely need someplace to park my liquid assets. Before we get started, George. I want you to know that I only deal with managers of firms. I prefer not to be handed off to a broker."

"I am sure I can accommodate you. How large an account do you anticipate opening at this time?"

"To be frank with you, I have amassed quite a fortune over the past nineteen years. Most of my capital came from oil and mineral holdings in Africa, Asia, and the Middle East. My initial deposit with your firm would be $800 million."

George Paler silently gasped. He did not want to look shocked. Maintaining his composure and poker face he said, "That should not be a problem. After all, this is Morgan Stanley. We are quite comfortable handing an account of that size."

Pompous ass! Let's get this done and let me get out of here, Peter thought to himself. "That is why I am here. Why don't we take care of the paperwork? I will have my bank, the Royal Bank of Scotland, make the necessary transfers and certify all the documents needed to move my money."

"That's fine," George said. He picked up the handset on his desk phone and pressed the intercom button. "Margery, could you please come in."

As Margery walked through the door, George rhetorically asked, "Margery, I believe you met Mr. Sanders?"

"Yes, I have."

"Margery, we are going to be handling Mr. Sanders's portfolio. Please prepare all the necessary forms he will need."

"Certainly, Mr. Paler."

Peter Sanders handed Margery his business card, which contained all his personal information.

"The only additional information I will need, Mr. Sanders, is your tax ID or Social Security account number," Margery said.

"Let me write it on the back of my card for you."

"Thank you. I shouldn't be more than a few minutes."

As Margery left the office, George said, "Can I get you anything, Peter? Coffee, water, or a soft drink? I'm sorry but it's too early in the day for anything stronger."

"No, thank you, I'm fine."

They made idle talk for a few minutes until Margery returned to the office with the forms. She handed them to her boss for his inspection. "Thank you, Margery." He looked over the forms and placed them on the desk in front of Peter. "If all the information is correct, all I will need is your signature in duplicate, and we can get started."

Peter examined the application and signed the forms. "I will need your routing numbers so my bank can complete the transfer," he said.

"I should have them for you in three days, if that's okay. We need seventy-two hours to open your account and run it through our compliance department. I will notify you when your account is opened with all the information you will need."

"That would be fine. George, I believe we will have a nice working relationship together. I'm certain it will not be a complicated one. I would love to chat with you further, but I do have another appointment."

"I understand. Maybe we can have lunch together some day?"

"Perhaps!" They shook hands, and he left.

Sanders left the building and walked two blocks south to 60 Wall Street. He found the public men's room in the lobby and entered it. When he exited it about two minutes later, his mustache and sideburns had been replaced with a pair of black-framed eyeglasses. His brown eyes were now green. He rode the elevator to the U.S. offices of Deutsche Bank. There he deposited another $380 million.

CHAPTER 11

Jack Rollins, walked into the London offices of Merrill Lynch, on King Edward Street. He was six feet one inch tall, with jet black hair combed straight back. His dark eyes seemed to stand out on his tan face. He was wearing a navy blue pin-striped suit. His jacket was buttoned. A red silk pocket square, which matched his tie, which concealed the buttons on his white shirt, was neatly folded in his breast pocket. Impeccably dressed, he could have stepped off the cover of Gentlemen's Quarterly magazine. As he approached the reception desk, the woman behind the desk couldn't help but notice him.

Taking a deep breath, she said, "Good day, sir. May I help you?"

"Yes, miss. I would like to meet with one of your investment counselors," he said as he handed her his business card.

"Anyone in particular?" she asked.

"No. I am new to your firm. It really doesn't matter."

"Please have a seat. I will have someone come out to meet you."

As Jack Rollins turned to walk toward the reception area, the receptionist quickly removed a compact from her purse. She used the mirror to check her teeth for signs of the lunch she had just eaten, check her make-up, and primp her hair. She returned the compact to her purse and dialed an extension on her telephone. After a brief conversation, she discreetly opened one more button on her blouse to expose more of her cleavage. She glanced at his business card once again to make sure she had his name correct. Rising from her chair, she hiked up her skirt a little to show more of her legs and walked around the desk to where Jack Rollins was seated in a high-backed, tufted leather chair.

"Mr. Rollins, Mr. Louis Harris will be with you shortly. Is there anything I can get you? A cup of tea perhaps, or water?"

"No thank you, miss…"

"Maureen—my name is Maureen," she interjected quickly.

"No, thank you, Maureen. I'm fine," he said, taking notice that she was being a little flirtatious.

She sauntered back to her desk, disappointed that he had not engaged her in more conversation.

About one minute later, a short stocky man about five feet eight inches tall weighing about 200 pounds, walked into the reception area. He was wearing a grey suit, the jacket of which was open, revealing a white shirt, whose buttons were straining against the weight behind them. His dark hair was disheveled, and it appeared as if he had just awakened from a nap. He spoke in a soft voice that did not seem to reflect his size. "Mr. Rollins?" he asked as he extended his hand.

Jack Rollins rose from his seat. "Yes. Mr. Harris, I presume?"

As both men shook hands, Louis Harris said, "Please call me Louis,"

"Only if you'll call me Jack." The two men chuckled.

"Let's go to my office. Can I offer you anything—a cup of tea or a soft drink?"

"No, thank you. Maureen was kind enough to offer me some refreshments earlier." *And probably more*, he thought to himself.

The two men walked down a short corridor to Louis's office. It was a small, cluttered, rectangular room about twelve by fourteen, which contained a large wooden desk. There was a wall of brown wood bookshelves on the wall behind the desk. They were built in and went from floor to ceiling. The lower shelves were cluttered with outdated business magazines and newspapers. On the wall adjacent to the desk was a matching credenza. Two leather armchairs that were in front of and facing the desk accompanied it. "Please, Jack, have a seat."

As he sat down in one of the chairs, Jack Rollins glanced around the room. *It appears this office belongs to the absent-minded professor,* he thought to himself. *This is just what I need—anonymity.*

"Louis, let me get right to the point. I have amassed a considerable sum of money in my short lifetime, most of which came from large inheritances and smart investments. I am moving from Philadelphia to the U.K. and want to move my assets with me. I am looking for a place to deposit and invest my money. However, I do not need any investment advice. I just need a place to park it where I can make my own investments without getting any advice from the firm. You, of course, will earn and receive any and all commissions for completing my transactions."

"I am sure we can accommodate you, Jack. How large an account do you wish to open?"

"My initial deposit would be 440 million pounds."

"Excuse me, did you say 440 million would be your initial deposit?"

"Yes, that is correct. There may be more later on, but for now 440 million should get us started."

After filling out the required paperwork, Jack Rollins walked out of the London office of Merrill Lynch just as he had walked in.

In the U.S., Europe, China, Japan, South America, and Canada, the scenario was the same. When the plan was complete, 873 brokerage accounts, with an average deposit of $410 million, were opened under different names. In total almost $358 billion was deposited into the world's stock markets. The process took eleven months to complete.

Things were beginning to take shape. Over the next sixteen months, more than one trillion dollars would quietly enter the global markets.

Seven days after his initial deposit with Prudential Securities, Ron Gilbert telephoned Sarah Dansk and asked her to purchase 200,000 shares of General Electric, 100,000 shares of Exxon Mobil, 200,000 shares of Verizon, 100,000 shares of Apple, and 100,000 shares of AMR, the parent company of American Airlines, at the market.

Similar transactions were being conducted at other brokerage firms around the world without raising a red flag. This was only the beginning.

CHAPTER 12

The economy of the world was growing. The United States was enjoying its lowest trade deficit in history. The Dow was at 24,600, and the NASDAQ was over 9,000. Unemployment in America was at 3.8 percent, and mortgages were under four percent. Home ownership was at a record high. The president's approval rating was at ninety-one percent, unheard of in previous administrations. To say the mood of the populace was elated would be an understatement.

Robert Prescott, soon to become the former president of the United States, would be free to do what he wished in his retirement. However, former presidents sometimes are busier than during their time in office. The hundreds and sometimes thousands of staff members they once had are reduced to a handful of people. Prescott's immediate task would be planning his presidential library and writing his memoirs. After that was completed, he would be free to go on speaking tours, play golf, or do whatever else he wanted. He and his vice president would have left the country in good condition.

As with most administrations, it was the vice president who was the beneficiary of the office of president, unless there were some missteps that caused some mistrust in the administration, party, or candidate.

That was not the case with the Prescott administration. Both he and Robert Amanti had behaved admirably. They shared the duties of the office with great care so they would not disturb the balance of power.

President Prescott handled most of the domestic issues while delegating matters of foreign relations to vice president Amanti. Amanti handled them commendably; especially when it came to the Middle East. He worked closely with his best friend, the secretary of state, Barry Melat. Melat helped to ensure that terrorism was no longer a concern and assisted the Arab world in building a strong coalition leading to the formation of the Islamic Union of Moslem Countries.

When Robert Amanti received his party's nomination for the office of president, it came as no surprise when he offered Barry Melat the opportunity to be his vice president.

With the U.S. economy strong, taxes low, unemployment low, and the world at peace, it was a certainty that Robert Amanti and Barry Melat would be elected in a landslide vote. When the final votes were counted, they had received over seventy-one percent of the popular vote, a record for any presidential election ever held.

President Amanti's inaugural speech was almost boring. He thanked his predecessor, President Prescott, and his administration for their magnificent job in helping to keep the world at peace and the economy flourishing. He promised more of the same. With the U.S. on a straight path of peace and prosperity, it appeared his administration would probably have an easy time of it.

When it came time to deliver his first State of the Union Address, all he had to do was show up and take his bows. There really wasn't much of a new agenda. All he needed to accomplish was to keep the status quo, and everything would be fine. He did speak of how proud he was of corporate America's role in keeping the economy growing and how they had continually contributed to the infrastructure of the nation. Corporations were becoming more community minded. It was almost like small town America 150 years ago, but on a much larger scale.

He was grateful that terrorism had been halted worldwide and was also grateful for the way nations were working with each other in the name of peace. He promised to continue to dialogue with America's friends across the oceans to improve life in the impoverished nations of the world. His final pledge was to ask Congress to cut defense spending by thirty percent and ask the joint session to deposit the savings into the Social Security fund, which had been privatized six years earlier but still had a deficit to make up. He received a thunderous standing ovation from both sides of the aisle with that proposal. The only question in many minds was, *Is he being naïve?*

CHAPTER 13

The ambassador from the Islamic Union, which included Saudi Arabia, Iran, Iraq, Yemen, Syria, Egypt, Jordan, Kuwait, Qatar, Libya and the Arab Emirates, called the White House requesting a meeting with President Amanti. After a quick review of the president's schedule, chief of staff Bertram Lane arranged a luncheon meeting.

Lane had been President Amanti's campaign manager. He was forty-eight years old and had lived in Washington, D.C. and been around politicians most of his adult life. Lane had been married for fourteen years. His wife was also an attorney, working for a Washington law firm. He was a brilliant jurist and a great administrator. Amanti and Lane had been friends for about ten years. Amanti had asked Lane to assume this role in the Oval Office a month before the election. That was how certain they were that they would win the election.

The following Tuesday, Ambassador Salaam Mamet and President Amanti met for lunch in the dining room of the West Wing. Present at the meeting were Chief of Staff Lane and Vice President Melat. The White House photographer was present to take a few photo op pictures but left shortly thereafter. The four men exchanged the usual complimentary remarks and lunched on salads made of Middle Eastern delights. The

White House kitchen staff was always cognizant of who was dining and prepared the menu accordingly.

The ambassador said, "Mr. President, as you know, my country is hosting the upcoming G-20 economic summit this spring. I am here today on behalf of his Excellency Abdul Faheem, who has instructed me to extend our formal invitation to you. As you know, his Excellency is also the president of the Union of Islamic Nations. Our ambassadors in the other nations who will be attending the summit will be delivering their invitations as well. As always, if you have any personal needs during your stay in my country, we will be more than happy to accommodate you. His Excellency fondly remembers the last time he was in America, when he was a guest of your predecessor. He believes it would only be fitting for you to accept his invitation to be his guest at the royal palace during the summit."

Looking toward his chief of staff and receiving an approval nod, the president said, "I do not see a problem with his kind invitation. Please assure his excellency that I cordially accept his hospitality."

"Thank you, Mr. President. I am sure he will be pleased."

They ended their meal with coffee and the Middle Eastern pastry baklava.

At the same time, invitations were being extended to the leaders of other nations, including Argentina, Australia, Brazil, Canada, China, France, Germany, India, Indonesia, Italy, Japan, South Korea, Mexico, Russia, South Africa, Turkey, and the United Kingdom. It was a formality that the host country extend invitations to the members who would be attending the summit.

After their meeting and lunch, which lasted about ninety minutes, Ambassador Mamet shook hands with Chief of Staff Lane, the vice president, and the president. His handshake with Vice President Melat seemed firmer and more direct than with the president and chief of staff. No one seemed to notice, however, except the two men. He then left the dining area and departed the White House. As the president turned and started to walk toward the oval office, he jokingly said to his chief of staff, "I hope the palace beds are more comfortable than the Lincoln Bedroom." They both chuckled.

CHAPTER 14

It was a sunny and clear April 4th, one year and seventy-two days into Robert Amanti's presidency, when he, Bertram Lane, eight members of his administrative staff, and eleven members of the White House press corps boarded Air Force One at Andrews Air Force Base. They were traveling to Saudi Arabia for the G-20 economic meeting of nations. Fourteen hours later, the president and his party deplaned at King Khalid International Airport in Riyadh, where they were met by President Faheem and three members of his cabinet. There was a military band playing a slightly off-key "Hail to the Chief." As they stood at attention, listening to the band finish, the president whispered to his chief of staff, "Next time we should bring the Marine Corps Band with us." Lane smiled.

The two leaders walked to the microphone that was set up at the end of the red carpet. Speaking in English with a slight Middle Eastern accent, President Faheem welcomed President Amanti and said he was eagerly looking forward to their meetings.

Faheem, a deeply religious man, had been born in Saudi Arabia. His father had been the minister of education, which was considered a high-level government job. His mother, as with most Saudi women, did not work. She stayed at home and cared for Faheem's three brothers and two sisters. Faheem was the oldest and most educated in the family. At the age of twenty-four he had completed a Master's Degree in Business from the London School of Economics. Upon returning home, he worked in the Saudi Treasury Office, where his duties included handling foreign investments. After several promotions he became involved with the Saudi government, helping to form the Islamic Union. His counterpart in the U.S. was then-secretary of state Barry Melat, whom he worked closely with. As a young man in his early teens he had traveled to Indonesia to take his religious training at the same Madrassa that Michael Haman attended, although they had never met and didn't know of each other. After developing the Islamic Union, Faheem was appointed as its president by a simple majority of the member nations. His appointment may have had something to do with the incredible wealth he had accumulated.

His fortune was believed to have been acquired legitimately. However, in the business world, just like in life, sometimes it is necessary to deal with individuals whose hands are not as clean as one would hope. Was this the case with Faheem?

The American president echoed Faheem's remarks. The two men shook hands and walked side by side to the waiting limousines. Noticing the planes of France, Germany, and Japan on the distant tarmac, surrounded by military guards, the president thought to himself, *It appears that some of our friends have already arrived at the party.* The seven-car processional drove to the presidential palace for a luncheon and an opportunity to get acquainted.

That evening 600 people attended a formal dinner party. The four leading members of the G-20 were seated with Faheem at the elevated dais in the banquet hall. They spoke among themselves as they dined. The other leaders were seated at the front row of tables, some with their spouses, who were attending, and their staff.

Besides President Amanti, the three predominant members of the G-20 on the dais were Chancellor Gephardt of Germany, President Frisse of France, and Charles Dunning, prime minister of Great Britain.

Gephardt, a native of Berlin, had been born fifty-six years earlier. A member of the Social Democratic Party of Germany, he had run a progressive government since his election nine years earlier. He had a close family and tried to maintain a balance between his public and private life. He was in the fourth year of his second five-year term as chancellor.

Seated next to him was President Jacques Frisse of France, who'd been born in Paris to a middle-class family. His mother was a social worker and his father a medical doctor, who had once run for office in local politics but failed. He has been single for the last twelve years since his divorce. He considered himself an atheist, and while respecting all religious practices, he had none of his own.

Frisse had lived in the United States for three years while a student at U.C.L.A. When he returned to France, immediately after graduating, he was employed as a counselor in the French Court of Audit, a quasi-judicial body of the French government charged with conducting financial and legislative audits of most public institutions, including the central government. He had been a member of the French Parliament for eleven years and was elected president the first time he ran. He had been re-elected two years earlier and was entering the third year of his second but last five-year term.

Charles Dunning was the leader of the Conservative Party of the British Parliament. He was a graduate of Brasenose College, in Oxford, with a degree in Philosophy and Politics. He was described by his professors as one of the brightest students they had known. At fifty-nine years of age, Dunning had been married for thirty-five years. He and his wife, Gwendolyn, were Protestants, and they had four children and three grandchildren. He had run for Parliament after working for the minister of defense for seven years. In the United Kingdom, the prime minister has no term limits. He is appointed by the monarch and remains in office so long as he can command the confidence of the House of Commons. Dunning had been the prime minister for the past six years.

The palace hall, which was about one-hundred-forty feet square, was decorated in a baroque style, with white marble walls. The floor was black, white, and tan marble, installed in a large diamond-shaped pattern. The walls were lined with twenty-four-carat gold columns, which rose from the floor to the twenty foot-high coffered ceiling. They were evenly spaced about twenty feet apart. Gold gargoyles adorned the arches over each doorway. Gold-framed mirrors were mounted on the walls between the archways. The ceilings were painted to mimic the frescoes of the

Sistine Chapel. Sixteen extremely large crystal chandeliers hung from the ceiling, symmetrically placed to light the room evenly. They weighed over 1,200 pounds each. The room appeared to be more like a museum than a banquet hall. One of the participants remarked that it resembled Catherine Palace in St. Petersburg, Russia. The room easily could hold 1,500 people for dinner; tonight it was set for 600. Besides the leaders of the G-20, their staff and press, there were about 250 guests of Faheem. Some were members of the Saudi royal family.

During dinner, President Faheem spoke. His remarks complimented the leaders who were present on the excellent job they were doing to maintain an orderly economic balance and peace in the world. He briefly mentioned the turmoil that the Middle East had gone through over the last fifty years, and how the new economic order had created peace and prosperity among the nations that were present, and the rest of the world. He particularly mentioned President Amanti, and the excellent job his administration was doing to continue peaceful relations with the Moslem nations.

President Amanti, representing the assembled group, briefly spoke. "I want to thank President Faheem and his cabinet for their hospitality. I hope the mutual trust the leaders here today have for each other and the Moslem world will last for generations to come. I am looking forward to our meetings tomorrow to further cement the members of this conference's friendships and relationships."

When the evening's festivities ended, the leaders exited the banquet hall for the brief walk together to the residence side of the palace, where President Amanti, his immediate personal staff, and the other leaders were staying. When they reached a large rotunda, Faheem stopped and spoke to the group.

"Gentlemen, please have a good evening. If there is anything you need during your stay, I have assigned a personal valet to each of you to attend to any and all of your needs."

"Thank you, your excellency," could be heard collectively from the group. Then the leaders dispersed through multiple corridors to their respective suites.

CHAPTER 15

After an informal breakfast the next morning, the assembled group met for a walk through the palace gardens. At the request of Faheem, the leaders met privately without any of their staff or press in attendance.

The stone paths meandered among some of the most spectacular topiaries they had ever seen. They were like living scenes. There was a group of six camels trimmed from hedges. From a distance they looked like a caravan traveling through an ancient desert. Another depicted the pyramids of Egypt.

President Amanti remarked, with some humor, "I will have to ask your gardener to come back with me to redo the White House Rose Garden."

"That could possibly be arranged," Faheem replied.

At the end of the seemingly never-ending gardens was a large mosque. Its five minarets were made of blue mosaic tile. Their cone-shaped spires were gilded in real gold. Their windows were made from brightly blue, red, and gold-colored stained glass. The morning sun was shining brightly, silhouetting the spires as they rose from the mosque. The call for prayer began to echo from its towers.

"Gentlemen, you must excuse me. It is time for my morning prayers. Please feel free to wander through our gardens. If there is anything you need, one of my assistants will get it for you. They are watching from the palace balconies. You merely have to wave your hand. I won't be more than fifteen minutes. Why don't you admire the work of my gardeners and reflect on the peacefulness of the day?"

"Thank you, your excellency," the group chorused.

As President Faheem walked towards the mosque, about sixty other men could be seen entering for their morning prayers.

The group dispersed throughout the gardens, some walking in pairs, talking among themselves.

President Amanti was seated alone on a concrete bench next to a bird feeder. As he watched, a small flock of about eight yellow canaries kept coming and going, picking up seeds with their beaks and flying off to their nearby perches, only to return again, chirping in song. A blue butterfly hopped from flower to flower in a nearby patch of yellow, white, and purple daisies. The president watched as its delicate blue wings seemed to catch the gentle breeze to help it along. He thought how fragile its powdered wings were. This suddenly brought back his youthful days when his father would remind him never to hold a butterfly by its wings because you could damage its protective coating. It seemed like a metaphor as he thought how fragile the world was. The air was fresh and smelled clean like new linens on a freshly made bed.

His daydreaming was interrupted as the leaders of the G-20 regrouped when Faheem returned from the mosque to join them.

"I am sorry for the interruption. As you know, Moslems pray five times daily."

"No interruption at all. But in our positions, do you think five times a day is enough?" Amanti said jokingly. The group chuckled.

"Gentlemen," Faheem said, "it is wonderful that we have had no wars or conflicts in the world in the last three decades. We have a wonderful legacy to leave our grandchildren and their children to come." His tone seemed vague.

"However, although there is a belief that there is total peace in the world, it is not one that Islam truly embraces. According to our Qur'an, there will never be absolute and complete peace until the entire world's population is converted to Islam, a belief that is widely held by every true Moslem in the world." His voice became stern. "For Islam to flourish, the Twelfth Imam must return to bless the world with total, everlasting peace. And, that cannot happen until the world's population is completely Islamic."

"What is wrong with the way the world is today?" the French president asked.

"Every nation is at peace with one another, world travel is unrestricted, there have not been any attacks by any group against another in, as you say, the last thirty years," echoed Germany's chancellor.

President Amanti chimed in. "We are at peace. Why change it?" He did not like the tone of Faheem's voice or the premise he was subscribing to. It was as though he were denying the state of the world, denying that there was peace at all, at least a peace that followed a Judeo-Christian belief, a peace that spoke of religious freedom, no matter what your belief was.

"I don't think you understand, Mr. President. It is not Moslem peace. It is your peace, it is a Western Judeo-Christian peace, not the peace that would give comfort to the Moslem world. We cannot live a proper and righteous life until the Twelfth Imam returns, and that will not occur until the entire world converts to Islam. It is written in the Qur'an and it is Mohammed's law. And it will be done." His last remarks were spoken with conviction, and in a raised voice.

The group seemed stunned. Shocked by what he was hearing, Robert Amanti responded. "You really do not believe the world will just acquiesce to your beliefs?" he asked rhetorically.

"Moslems are commanded to fight nonbelievers until they are either dead, converted to Islam, or in a permanent state of conquest under Moslem domination. Allowing people of other faiths to live and worship independently of Islamic rule is not an option. Gentlemen, unfortunately for you and the rest of the world, you no longer have a choice. Come with me. I want to show you something."

Robert Amanti looked toward his Secret Service agents, who were standing on the other side of the garden, and nodded toward them. As two of his protectors started to step forward, Faheem noticed them and said, "You will not need your guards. You are safe here. This is a place of peace. We no longer resort to violence. We have found an alternative way to bring total peace to the world, as you will soon learn."

The president shook his head from side to side. His security stood down.

The group entered the mosque. As the American president's eyes adjusted to the dim light, he began to focus on the men inside who had finished their prayers. As they were rising from their prayer rugs, he seemed to recognize one of the men. Dressed in a traditional Moslem thobe, he was about twenty-five feet away from the president and walking toward him, his right hand extended to shake the president's.

"Good morning, Mr. President," the silhouetted voice said.

As his eyes focused, Robert Amanti recognized the face of Ian Sellers, CEO of Verizon, the largest telecommunications corporation in the world. Sellers controlled over ninety-four percent of the entire flow of electronic communications. His company owned the controlling interest of every telephone network worldwide.

Ian Sellers had begun working for Verizon as a wire splicer while he was going to college, back when the company was still New York Telephone. He worked his way up through the company, becoming executive vice president, and finally taking the reins as CEO twenty-two years later. He held a business degree and an MBA from Columbia University. He was married and had two children, a married son, and a married daughter.

Ian himself lived in suburban New York but maintained an apartment in the city. He also had a home in Palm Beach, Florida. He had been a close personal friend of President Amanti for over twenty years and had been one of his biggest supporters, both emotionally and financially, in all his campaigns over the years. He was a man of complete confidence in himself, resolute in his business dealings, which was what had made him the success he was.

"Ian, what are you doing here?" the puzzled president asked.

"You will soon understand, Mr. President." Sellers winked at the president while shaking his hand. When Amanti released his grip of Sellers's hand, he felt a folded piece of paper in it. He held it against the palm of his hand with his thumb and quickly placed it in his jacket pocket.

Suddenly, one by one, each of the worshippers stepped forward and extended their hands to the assembled group. There were Steven Moslek, CEO of Moslek Logistics Inc., the director of all ocean, air, and railroad freight, John Malcolm, the president and CEO of the largest auto manufacturer. His conglomerate accounted for over eighty percent of all vehicles in the world. Then came William Guess, the mega software developer with almost ninety-three percent of the controlling interest in the industry. He also was accountable for about eighty-eight percent of the world's email.

As the men stepped forward and greeted the assembled group, they shook each leader's hand in greeting. A sudden wave of nausea came over Robert Amanti. His breathing became heavy as his mind filled suddenly with thoughts of fear and confusion. It was like walking in the woods in total darkness. Every sound in the night was more frightening than the last. It wasn't the dark he was afraid of but what might be in it. He was no longer at peace as he had been just thirty minutes earlier in the palace garden.

Fifty-seven men, one by one, stepped forward. They were the most powerful corporate leaders in the world. They controlled everything from auto manufacturing to energy, from food distribution to pharmaceutical manufacturing, even the utility industries were represented. *What does all this mean?*, he wondered to himself. Why would all these powerful men be here in a mosque praying the Qur'an together? He could not comprehend what was happening. He felt as though his air supply were being cut off, and momentarily he became disoriented. He had to remind himself that he was the leader of the most powerful nation in the world. *I must regain control of my thoughts,* he told himself. *Let me see how this plays out.*

The other members of the G-20 also looked totally confused and stunned. The feelings he had seemed to be shared by the other leaders. You could see it in their faces. *But Sellers winked at me,* he thought to himself. *What could that mean? And what could be on the paper he secretly handed me?* He dared not look at it now for fear of being discovered.

Faheem stepped forward, took the American president by the shoulder, and guided him toward a door in the rear of the mosque. "Gentlemen, please," he said, motioning the group to follow along. As the corporate leaders walked behind, you could hear whispers throughout the group.

They entered a large conference room that was about twenty by forty feet. It contained a twenty-two-foot-long conference table with twenty-six upholstered armchairs around it, twelve on each side and one at each end. "Please be seated," Faheem said. "I know you seem confused at what is happening, gentlemen. Please let me explain. I will tell you everything you need to know."

Faheem stood at the head of the table, waiting for the group to be seated. He took his seat, poured himself a glass of water from the pitcher in front of him, took a drink, and began to speak. "Gentlemen, let me tell you why the CEOs of the largest corporations in the world are gathered here. As you know, they control everything that is vital for the survival of life on earth. These powerful men control every industry."

The group was silent. It was so quiet in the room that you could almost hear your own heart beating. The assembled members were apprehensive about what was to come.

Faheem continued. "The reason they are here with us is, I instructed them to be here."

"What do you mean, *instructed* them to come?" England's prime minister asked.

"I instructed them because they all work for me. I and the people I represent own the controlling interest in all their companies, and they are all true believers of Islam. They are all Moslems, a secret that has been kept for years."

"That's impossible," Amanti said. "I have known Ian Sellers of Verizon for years. Our families celebrate Christmas together."

"And then he goes home and prays the Qur'an for forgiveness," Faheem responded.

"I don't believe you. This is preposterous," Jacques Frisse, the French president, said.

Chancellor Gephardt of Germany echoed, "It is impossible. Why would these men acquiesce to you? Who do you think you are?"

The group was abuzz with chatter. It sounded like a theater in the moments before the house lights dimmed. Faheem let them chat among themselves for about two minutes, then called the group to order. "Gentlemen, please," he said sternly. His voice was the loudest one in the room. The room fell silent once again.

Faheem continued, "The plan to rule the world economically was conceived during the 1990s. We first had to create fear among the democratic nations by terrorizing them. The first explosion in 1993 at the World Trade Center in New York was the first offensive act to get the Americans to react. Unfortunately, Mr. President, your country's president at the time was weak and treated it as a criminal act, not an act of terrorism. We kept taunting your nation with other acts of terrorism, but no matter what we did, your president remained weak. Even when the U.S.S. Cole was bombed, he did nothing. We had your presidents convinced that Iraq's Saddam Hussein had weapons of mass destruction. We even convinced Saddam to set up terrorist training camps. Your CIA was aware of them, as well as of the WMDs. When the intelligence was passed on to President Bush, there was nothing he could do. There were no other acts of terrorism that needed to be executed.

Osama Bin Laden was a stooge who took his orders from us. Unfortunately, he became a loose cannon. We couldn't control him. He decided to form his own group. Bin Laden wanted to take over the world, but he lacked the knowledge or the money. When he struck America in 2001, he unknowingly helped us by diverting attention from our economic strategy.

This led to the Iraq War, which had the American people focused on the war on terror as we secretly bought up your country's economy. President Bush, at the time, was taking credit for turning around America's economy. What your people did not know is that we were bolstering it with unbelievable capital we were secretly infusing into corporate America. We had begun our plan in 1993 during the Clinton administration. During the Bush administration we managed to help keep your rate of unemployment low and your GDP high.

By the way, Mr. President, just for your information, Iraq did have WMDs. Saddam moved them to Syria while he was stalling the weapons inspectors. Israel destroyed most of them, along with the nuclear reactor Syria was completing in 2007 when they sent an air strike into Syria. Cunning little country, that Israel. They have been like a pimple on a camel's ass—no matter how much the beast scratches, it won't go away." *That will change soon*, he thought to himself. "Knowing that the only way we could defeat our enemies was to hit them in their wallets, we had to control the economies of the world."

He turned and looked at President Cho of China and said, "India's and your demands for oil by 2009 was outrageous. We knew that Saudi Arabia had only about twelve years left before our wells ran dry. Therefore, we secretly purchased the stock of all the major oil companies in the world. We then merged them and formed the largest oil conglomerate in America. Our U.S. affiliates convinced the U.S. government to drill in Alaska and off the Gulf Coast, convert coal to oil, and remove the oil from the sands of Canada and the shale of Colorado, while at the same time keeping the environment safe so as not to upset the environmentalists, who hate big oil. We then made sure the Excel Pipeline was approved, and we diverted that oil as well. The total amount of oil from these sources could run the world for the next 500 years. At the same time, we purchased the utility companies in America and Europe and developed 146 nuclear power plants to reduce the cost of energy and reduce greenhouse gases.

All the time you thought you were doing it yourselves. However, it was us. You thought you were the new oil barons of the world, Mr. President," he said smugly.

Robert Amanti felt sick, as though his stomach were about to give back the morning's feast. He felt a pain in his abdomen as if someone were twisting his intestines. It appeared he wasn't the only one in the room who felt that way.

"At the same time, we were buying the airlines, railways, shipping lines, and trucking companies. We wanted to control the movement of freight around the world. We also own forty-eight percent of the farmland in America and Canada. The beef industry in your country," as he turned and looked at Charles Dunning of England, "Mr. Prime Minister, belongs to us, as well as your transportation and shipping industry.

"We own almost every auto manufacturer and telecommunications company in the world.

So you see, gentlemen, we control the economy of the world. There is nothing you can do about it. Once our plan was in place, we knew we would not need violence to convert the world to Islam. Our Qur'an tells us to convert the population of the world through any means possible, even death to the resisters who will not convert. We found a better way. We decided that the violence had to stop if we were to take over the world. We had to lull your governments into feeling secure, even though you may now believe it was a false sense of security. You believed the Qur'an was like Hitler's *Mein Kampf,* only we did not follow it, as Hitler followed his book. We reinterpreted it to suit our needs. All of your so-called Islamic experts were busy reading the Qur'an to find out our next move. Instead, we changed it, trading blood for money."

The assembled group of world leaders could not believe what they were hearing. It was as though all the members of the G-20 were all having a simultaneous nightmare. They started to whisper among themselves. *Lunatic* and *psychopath* could be heard under the leaders' breaths. However, the operative feeling among those assembled was fear.

"Gentlemen, let me assure you that no one here will be harmed. I will present my plan to you shortly. The CEOs you met who are assembled here are all Moslems. Some are pure, born as Moslems, while others are converts. In any event, they all have the same beliefs. They believe that the conversion of the world is necessary for the Twelfth Imam to return."

"I know most of these men personally. I have never known them to be of the Moslem faith," President Amanti interjected.

"They have been engaged in the practice of *taqiyya and kitman,* our doctrine of religious deception, a Moslem practice of being a pretender of other faiths to defend and further the cause of Islam," Faheem stated with confidence. "They don't have to hide any longer. We want to continue the peace that the world is experiencing. The only difference is that we want to continue it under the Islamic flag.

"After lunch, I will lay out the plan we have developed, which I think you will find very interesting. Please, join me in the palace dining room. And if you have any thoughts of calling your embassies or governments, all communications have been blocked until further notice. So, gentlemen, for the time being, you are my captive audience." He was acting arrogant.

CHAPTER 16

After the lunch service, which for the most part was left untouched, Faheem stood up and told the group to reassemble in the larger banquet hall they had used for the opening dinner. When the members filed in, they joined the CEOs who had been praying in the mosque earlier that morning. They were seated at the front of the room facing the assembled leaders of the G-20. The room still retained the odors of the dinner that had been served the night before. Faheem stood before the assembled group and began his prepared speech. When he spoke, his voice was once again stern, and so were his words.

"Gentlemen, our plan is very simple. You will return to your countries and explain to your Congresses, Parliaments, and whatever ruling parties are in your control that 180 days from now the flags of all your nations will be changed to the Islamic flag. Your governments will now be under our rule. All your embassies will be closed. There will be no need for them anymore. In time your churches, synagogues, and all other houses of worship will all be converted to mosques. There will be only one religion in the world: Islam!

If you do not acquiesce to our demands, we will immediately begin to cut off all services and products that you need to sustain your daily lives, which includes transportation, energy, food, water, and any other things you need. If need be, we will starve you into submission."

"You are a madman," said Gephardt of Germany.

"You can't be serious," the French president echoed.

"Of course I am serious," Faheem said. "How will your people react when we cut off your flow of wine?" he asked, while laughing.

President Amanti stood and said, "Do you really think you can get away with this mad scheme? Who do you think you are?"

Faheem spread his arms wide and acknowledged the CEOs on both sides of him with a wave of his hands and said, "These men all work for me. They take their orders from me. And, most of all, they are devoted members of Islam and our need to rule the world so the Twelfth Imam will appear from occultation. They will do whatever they are commanded to do. They will do it to their death if necessary. This shall be the final act to complete the caliphate we began fifty years ago—or, as you say in the Western world, the final nail in the coffin. As it was written, it shall be done. You can call this our Economic Jihad." He sounded as if he felt all powerful, as though he had just thrown the winning pass in the Super Bowl.

Faheem continued, his voice becoming softer. "Gentlemen, as you leave this room, you will each receive a bound book containing directions of how you will proceed when you return to your country. Each one has been prepared for you personally, depending upon your governmental structure. Study it wisely. It will be your guide to turning over control of your country to Islam. We trust that your people will be convinced to comply with our demands through your words and actions. We don't want to be forced into convincing them with drastic actions, although if need be we will.

Nothing will change. Your citizens will still come and go as before. They will still maintain their status in their communities. They will continue with their employment. The only difference is they will be under Islamic rule and Sharia Law.

One more thing: There will be only one currency in the world. It will be the dinar, backed by all the gold in your reserves, which you will turn over to our treasury." With that said, President Faheem completed his statement by calling the conference of the G-20 to an end and dismissing the group to return to their respective nations.

The assembled leaders left the room in anguish. As they passed through the door of the banquet hall, they were each handed a leather-bound book that was tied with a wide leather strap. The name of each country was engraved on its cover.

The members of the G-20 gathered in the corridor and spoke among themselves. It was actually incoherent chatter, as each of the leaders tried to talk at the same time. There was disbelief and fear about what they had just experienced and heard.

Charles Dunning of Great Britain held up his hands to silence the group and said loudly and sternly, "Gentlemen please, please, this is not getting us anywhere. We need to be rational and think this through. I am as sickened, upset, and concerned as each of you at what we were presented. The situation we are facing is reprehensible and immoral, to say the least, but we can't go off without a plan. And this is not the place to formulate or discuss one. We have six months. I suggest we go back to our respective governments and try to come up with an option for what we must do in a unified manner. However, we must be careful about whom we confide in, because if any of this becomes disclosed beyond our closest confidantes, there could be pandemonium in our cities—and that would be the least of it.

"Please, I implore each of you to choose wisely regarding whom you share this knowledge with. I believe we must somehow meet together to formulate a strategy to combat this madman and his group. And I believe it must be soon. Please, let us be smart about this. Let's leave this place and realize that we may have been complacent in some way by letting ourselves and our government be lulled into believing that these people could be our friends. Please let us pray for guidance."

The assembled group circled, put their arms around each other's shoulders and, led by Chancellor Gephardt of Germany, asked the good Lord for guidance. The leaders agreed to speak via a secure conference call in three days, after they had had time to digest what was in each of their manuals. They vowed not to speak of this to anyone until they had spoken as a group. They then left to gather their belongings and leave for the airport.

As they walked through the corridors, there was silence and a stillness that left the air difficult to breathe. It wasn't the heaviness of the air but the anxiety and fear each were feeling—fear of unknown consequences and what might follow.

One by one, the planes that had brought them to what they had thought was going to be a conference of peace taxied out to the runways and left as they had come.

CHAPTER 17

Twelve years earlier, Michael Haman was preparing to enter the Wharton School of Business at the University of Pennsylvania. A brilliant and outstanding student, he completed his high school education with honors and also took some honors college classes before his seventeenth birthday. His thirst for knowledge would propel him through four years of college with straight A's.

However, life wasn't an easy ride. He became angry and rebellious. When he and his mother left Indonesia after his father's death and returned to Atlanta, Michael found it difficult to adjust to life without a father figure to guide him.

Sylvia Haman loved her son more than life itself. Even so, it's a difficult task being a single mother, especially to a son. There are so many simple things in life that women take for granted when there is a father in the home. Little things like learning how to shave or tying a tie are not things you learn from your mother. But somehow she muddled through it.

The big things like how to handle reaching puberty and what to do with those sexual urges were not so simple, so she let the library fill in the blanks in that department. She found a host of books he could read. Between the books and Michael's older classmates, she believed he could learn them on his own.

He had trouble adjusting to school, so his mother decided to home school him. He needed more structure and couldn't find it in a public school environment. When a letter arrived in the mail two months later informing her that Michael was entitled to receive a full scholarship to attend a private school from a fund that had been established by Alan's employer, she was totally surprised. She was unaware such a generous fund existed.

Because he was extremely smart, it was not much of a problem for Michael to start his new curriculum mid-semester. It seemed that the strict policies of a private education helped him lose his rebellious attitude. It did not take him long to catch up on his studies. He became immersed in his classes and had a thirst for knowledge. It may have been his way of dealing with the loss of his father. Michael believed his father was watching over him, guiding his every move. He missed him so much. The next year Michael entered high school. Once again he found himself in a private school environment, paid for by the generosity of Ameri-Pro.

It was no surprise when Michael excelled through school and graduated with honors. His mother was extremely proud of him. At his graduation she told him how proud she was. As she hugged him tightly, she said, "I wish your father could be here to see you. You have grown into a wonderful young man. I miss him so."

"I know, Mother. So do I. But he will always be with me, Mom. I will never forget him. He is part of my soul." They both had tears in their eyes as they walked from the ceremony.

Michael had a penchant for business. With his exceptional grades it was no surprise when his first choice for college was realized. He was accepted to the University of Pennsylvania's school of business on a full scholarship. Even his books were paid for.

Michael's roommate was eighteen-year-old Amir Ahren, also a business major. They shared many classes together. Amir was from New York City. He was about five feet eleven inches tall, about 180 pounds, with dark brown hair and brown eyes, and an olive complexion. He appeared to be from somewhere else than America. Amir told Michael that his grandparents, whom he never knew, were from Jordan. Michael thought to himself, *That explains his dark complexion.* Amir had come to the U.S. when he was fourteen and attended the Rhodes School. His father was a widower. "My mother died when I was nine. Dad travels around the world for business. He's an international business consultant. I don't get to see him much except when he's in New York on business. Now that I'm in Philadelphia, if I see him a few times a year it will be a lot," he explained. "But we're close. If it weren't for the Internet and cell phones, I would probably never see or speak to him."

"My dad died when I was eleven," Michael told Amir. "Maybe we should introduce them to each other." They both laughed.

Amir walked with confidence and spoke with an air of intelligence. He also had a thirst for knowledge. Perhaps that's why he and Michael became good friends. They studied together, socialized together, and could be seen in the library almost daily. They took their studies very seriously and shared a perfect 4.0 grade point average. Yet they did not feel competitive with each other. They respected one another and soon realized that they would probably be friends for life. Both dated co-eds at school, but nothing of those relationships became serious.

In their second year at school, Michael and Amir applied for and were granted membership into the Universities Economics Club. A year later they were elected president and vice president of the club, respectively.

About one month into the beginning of their junior year, Amir told Michael he was going to New York City for the weekend to visit his dad, who was in the city on business. "I can't wait. I haven't seen him in almost seven months."

"That's great!" Michael exclaimed.

"Why don't you come along? I'm sure you guys would get along great. We have plenty of room in our apartment."

"Thanks, but you guys haven't seen each other in a while. I'm sure you have a lot of catching up to do. I have enough to keep me busy here."

"Okay, but don't miss me too much," Amir said while laughing.

"Believe me, I won't. It will be nice to have peace and quiet for a change. Go and enjoy yourself. I want to call my mom and catch up. I haven't spoken with her in two weeks."

When he returned on Sunday evening from New York, Amir walked into their dorm room and said, "You missed a great time. You know who we had dinner with last night?"

"Was she tall, blonde, and dumb?" Michael's sense of humor was showing.

"Actually, no. Brown hair, and she was a he! Does the name Ian Sellers mean anything to you?"

"Sounds familiar. Why do I know that name?"

"Because you saw him on the cover of last month's *Fortune* magazine. The senior executive vice president at Verizon, the largest telecommunications company in the world."

"How did you pull that one off? Now I *am* sorry I wasn't there."

"I have a surprise for you. You're going to meet him. He's going be in Philadelphia next week at the meeting of a secret economic society known as the Samson and Delilah Society. He asked me to attend."

"You're joking?"

"No joke. He said I could bring a friend as long as he was an 'A' student in business. I couldn't think of anyone, so I thought I would ask you," he said jokingly. "I was told that they only accept students in their junior year and above with perfect 4.0s. They have interesting speakers and work on international economic problems that they try to solve. I was also told it was a secret society and not to mention it to anyone. Want to check it out and see what it's all about?"

"Are you kidding? I wouldn't miss the opportunity!"

The following week both boys traveled to an old, nondescript brownstone building in the heart of Philadelphia. They were met outside by Ian Sellers. He was forty-five years old, six feet tall, and slender, about 190 pounds, with brown hair and green eyes. He was dressed in a dark blue suit, with a white shirt and red-and-white-striped tie.

"Amir! It's good to see you again. Welcome!" Acknowledging Michael, he said, " This must be your friend Michael who you spoke so highly of." Extending his hand he added, "I'm glad to meet you. Nice to have you attend our meeting."

"No, it's my pleasure, Mr. Sellers. You are a legend in the telecommunications world."

"Thank you, Michael. Please call me Ian. Mr. Sellers is my dad."

They all chuckled.

They walked up the gray concrete steps, which were lined with wrought iron railings, to a large, dark wood door with a large door knocker in the middle. It was heavy, made of brass, and had the head of a lion on it. Above it was a peephole.

Ian led the boys inside to a vestibule. The walls were paneled in oak wainscoting, which was finished in a lustrous light brown stain. The paneling extended halfway up the walls and was topped with a chair railing. Oatmeal-colored grass cloth wall covering followed the rest of the wall to meet the old-fashioned tin ceilings in their natural color. They looked like they had been there for centuries. The ceiling was adorned with a row of light fixtures that resembled hanging opaque glass salad bowls adorned with brass trim. The floors were wide oak boards that creaked with every step you took. *It would be hard for someone to sneak into this place at night with noisy floors like these*, Michael thought.

They walked down the hallway to a large room that was about thirty feet wide by fifty feet long. It appeared that three rooms had been combined to make one large meeting room. The room's décor was the same as that of the entranceway. The room contained a total of ten windows, six on the side of the room that backed an outside wall, and four on the front wall of the brownstone. They were covered with window curtains that matched the wall coverings to conceal the inside activity from the outside world.

There were some platters of deli sandwiches and cheese with crackers set out on a table on the side of the room. Another cloth-covered table contained pitchers of water, iced tea, and soft drinks. "Help yourselves. I'm sorry, but we don't serve alcohol," Ian said.

"No problem," Amir said.

"Amir didn't give me many details what this club is all about," Michael said questioningly.

"It's really not a club. We call it a society. Our members are all current and former business and economic majors. The membership doesn't consist only of students but some of the most important executives and CEOs in business. Some are retirees who have remained members after they left their positions. Some of our members have gone on to political careers. Every one of our members is extremely successful. What we try to do is connect to the major business and political leaders in the world to improve society through economics and business. We believe that our members are the sharpest business and economic minds in the world."

"Very interesting," Michael said.

"The purpose of our society will become clear as you listen this evening. One thing I want to caution you about, though: If you were to join us or not—that is, if you are asked and accepted as members—everything you see, hear, and do here is in complete secrecy. Even your attendance at this meeting will be kept secret," Ian said.

"Have you heard of the Skull and Bones Society at Yale? We're similar to them, only they're autonomous; we are not. We have an organization with a hierarchy that, although we are democratic in nature, guides us through our mission."

"What is that mission?" Michael asked.

"To become the economic leaders of the world."

"You don't mean world domination?" Michael asked.

"No! But it would be nice," Ian answered laughingly. "Come, let's go inside."

The meeting room was filled with about fifty people, mostly important business leaders. Everyone seemed to know each other. Ian introduced Michael and Amir to so many people it was hard to keep track of their names. There were a few younger members who they believed were other students, but Michael and Amir didn't recognize any of them. Most of the attendees were older and were dressed in business suits. They seemed to be in their forties and fifties.

The meeting was called to order by a middle-aged gentleman who never introduced himself. He didn't have to. Everyone seemed to know who he was. He started with a few announcements, mostly of members who had been promoted within their professions or had moved on to senior positions with other companies. The leader went around the room asking the members present if they had any new business.

Ian stepped forward and proudly introduced his guests for the evening and praised them for their high academic achievements. "I hope after this evening's presentation they consider joining our society to help advance our mission. Let's welcome them in friendship."

As the members applauded their introduction, Michael felt a little embarrassed. Amir seemed to take it in stride.

Michael and Amir became aware, during the meeting, that this was the place to be if they wanted to find good business contacts and great employment when they finished school.

Ian asked the boys to stay a few minutes after the meeting ended. They were seated in the rear of the room when Ian approached and sat in a chair in front of them. Turning around to face them, he asked, "So, what do you think of our little group?"

"It appeals to me very much," Michael answered. "Your structure and mission are appealing." Speaking for both of them he continued. "How do we proceed from here?"

"It's simple. We do a complete due diligence on your background, grades, social networking, and anything we believe might tarnish your future. Not only your future as members, but your future in a corporate environment. Members of this group have gone on to become some of the most powerful business and political leaders in the world. Most of our members' future successes are based on the society's recommendations. We have a huge reputation to maintain, and the last thing we want is to tarnish it. From what I already know about both of you, I don't foresee any problem. However, before we begin our process we have an admissions committee that will interview you. If there is anything in your background that you believe would hamper your joining us, you can discuss it during the interview process. Just to let you know, if we believed you would not be right for us, you wouldn't have been invited to attend this evening. So I really don't believe there would be a problem."

"It all sounds fine to me," Amir said.

"Count me in," Michael echoed.

"Great!" Ian said. "Now, if you don't have any questions, let's call it a night. I'm sure you have early classes tomorrow. You'll hear from us shortly."

"Good night," both boys echoed, as they shook Ian's hand and left.

"And remember, you were never here," Ian stated ardently.

CHAPTER 18

Three days later, both boys received a text message asking them to call a telephone number that evening between 8:00 and 9:00. The number began with a 212 area code, which they recognized as New York City. When they called from their room about 8:15, the boys were eager in anticipation of what would transpire. The person on the other end answered by saying, "This is Steven Moslek."

Moslek was fifty-five years old and had been married for twenty-nine years. He and his wife, Susan, had met at Columbia, where they both attended. She was an art major; he studied business administration. After graduation, Steven took a position with a large trucking firm as Director of Logistics. Then he went back to school to study for his MBA and attended the executive MBA immersion program at Columbia. Susan continued on and received her Masters in Art History. She was a curator at Christie's Auction House in New York. They married during the second semester of Steven's graduate program. Within four years he was offered a chance to buy into his company. Through the help of the society, he was able to obtain the necessary funds to purchase the entire business.

Soon after, he became involved in ocean freight and then went on to air cargo. Now the company was the largest logistics corporation on the planet. Steven and Susan had two children, both boys. Each had his MBA. The older son, Lester, worked for Steven, running the shipping lines. The younger son, Gary, was an investment counselor for Credit Suisse.

Is this Michael or Amir?"

"I'm Michael. Amir is with me."

"Are you boys alone?"

"Yes!"

"If you would put this call on speaker, I could speak to both of you together."

Michael put the call on speaker, and both boys said, "Okay, we're here."

"I'm in charge of the search and admissions committee for the society you gentlemen were interested in joining."

The boys realized that he never used the name of the society, so they knew not to mention it either.

"Does your schedule permit you to travel to New York City this weekend so we can have a talk about your future?"

"Sure!" Amir said.

"I have nothing else I have to do," Michael said.

"That's great. How's Saturday about noon? We could meet at my office in the financial district. You could take the train in from Philly and a taxi to my office. We'll pay your expenses."

"That all sounds fine to me," Amir said. "I'm sure I can speak for Michael, and I'm sure we'll be there together."

"Works for me," Michael said.

"Good! Let me text you the address. Oh—and by the way, I have arranged for you to stay the night at the Sherry Netherland Hotel, opposite Central Park, so pack an overnight bag. Make sure to pack at least one business outfit. I want you to join me and some of my friends for dinner that evening. You can return on Sunday afternoon, if that's okay."

"Sounds fine," the boys said in unison.

"Good I'm looking forward to meeting you again. I didn't have time to speak with you the other evening. Have a good night."

"You too," Amir answered for both of them. Then, after disconnecting, he turned to Michael and asked, "What do you think?"

"I'm excited," Michael answered. "I can't wait until Saturday. By the way, did you notice he never mentioned the name of the club?"

"Yeah, I did."

About five minutes later, Amir received a text message. It simply said, "2 Broadway, Suite 3201, 12:00 P.M."

CHAPTER 19

After a ninety-minute Amtrak ride, which took them into New York's Pennsylvania Station, they hailed a taxi for the twenty-five-minute ride to 2 Broadway. When the cab pulled to the curb, a female passenger exited. She was dressed to the nines in a short black skirt with a red satin blouse and black four-inch heels. The boys could smell her pungent perfume as she walked past them. They entered the taxi, sliding their small carry-on bags across the seat, piling them on top of each other. The odor of the woman who had just gotten out of the taxi still permeated the air inside the cab.

They arrived at their destination and proceeded into the vast marble lobby toward a uniformed guard sitting behind an enclosed circular station. He was wearing a grey uniform consisting of trousers that were held in place by a black patent leather belt, which pressed the waistband against his shirt, which was pressed with military pleats. It held a square silver badge with a name tag under it that read "Harris." "May I help you gentlemen?" he asked.

Amir answered for both of them. "We're here to see Mr. Steven Moslek."

"Yes, he's expecting you. Here are your visitor's passes." He handed them two plastic laminated passes on lanyards to wear. As the boys placed them around their necks, the guard said, "Take the second bank of elevators on your left.

"Thank you," they said in unison.

As they walked toward the elevator, their footsteps echoed with every step across the vast marble lobby. They could hear the guard on the telephone notifying Steven that they were on their way up.

They rode the carpeted, mahogany-paneled elevator directly to the 32nd floor without any stops along the way. When the stainless steel doors opened, they revealed a large office lobby entrance. They were met by Steven Moslek and, to their surprise, Ian Sellers.

"Welcome, gentlemen. It's good to see you again," Ian said. "This is Steven Moslek. I don't know if you had the chance to meet him last week, so I will make the formal introduction now."

They all shook hands and proceeded into a huge corner conference room, which contained a one-piece oak conference table large enough to hold thirty for dinner. It was surrounded by twenty-four evenly placed high-backed leather chairs, which were on steel casters. Curious, Michael asked, "How did they get this table into this room?"

"It was delivered first. They built the room around it," Steven answered.

The two outside walls were all glass, which overlooked Battery Park, Staten Island, the Statue of Liberty, and New Jersey. When you looked north, you looked straight at the new World Trade Tower, which had been completed twelve years earlier. The view was breathtaking. The walls were decorated with ten framed poster-size photos of large freight container ships and tankers.

Noticing that Michael and Amir were looking at the photos, Steven said, "That's only part of our fleet. The other ninety-one ships are hanging throughout the rest of our offices. We occupy the top three floors of this building. Our airplane fleet is hanging in our London offices. Our freight trains reside in Phoenix."

Amir seemed flabbergasted at the number of transport vehicles Steven bragged of. "How much freight do you move each year?" he asked.

"A lot. Last year our total volume was over $950 billion. This year we expect to move more than $1.3 trillion. We are the largest freight carriers in the world."

"Maybe in the universe," Amir added. "Until they find a ship on Mars, you could probably get away with saying that."

"I like you already," Steven said while laughing.

Looking out the glass walls, Michael asked, "How do you get any work done in here with this view?" He smiled as he posed the question.

"It's simple. We close the curtains," Steven answered. With that said, he pushed a button on a remote transmitter, and two curtains moved, one from each side of the walls, to conceal the view. "We want your undivided attention, so let's block out the outside world for a little while and get started," he added. "Please take a seat."

Michael and Amir sat next to each other on the side of the table, facing one of the outside walls. Steven and Ian sat opposite them, leaving two chairs between them. Steven spoke first. "What did you think of our little society meeting the other night?"

"Very interesting," Michael answered for both of them. "To be honest, Amir and I discussed the group after we arrived back at our dorm that evening and came to the conclusion that it is where we want to be. We believe the group can help us with our career path."

"It can, but it's not a one-way street. You'll learn that membership comes with a price. You have to give as much as you get from it," Ian said. "You will learn that givers gain. The more you put into it, the more you'll reap the rewards. And the rewards can be very fruitful and endless."

"How do we proceed?" Amir asked enthusiastically.

"We already have. You were asked to come here under what you might say were false pretenses. This is not going to be an interview process. We have already done our due diligence on both of you and have decided to ask you to join the Samson and Delilah Society. Based on what we know about you, we believe you will be a great asset to us," Steven said happily.

"Wow! I don't know what to say," Michael said with vigor in his voice.

"Thank you," Amir added. "Where do we begin?"

"Well! Let's give you a little history of the society," Ian said. "We are a secret society. Much like Skull and Bones at Yale, we exist but we don't, if you know what we mean. The few people who are suspicious of our existence are plagued with curiosity. No one speaks of the society except members to each other, and they do it with caution. Numerous media outlets have tried to uncover us, to no avail.

"Our members consist of CEOs of Fortune 100 companies, leading economic advisors, and political leaders all over the world. Similarly, just like former President George W. Bush and former U.S. Senator and Secretary of State John Kerry were members of the Skull and Bones Society, some very prominent political figures in America and the world are members of the Samson and Delilah Society. For example, you may not have recognized him, but the gentleman standing toward the rear of the room in the blue pin-striped suit at last week's meeting was the current secretary of state, Barry Melat. I would have introduced you, but he left before the meeting ended. If you become members of the society you will be privy to many prominent people. As an aside, Bush and Kerry were the only two members of the Skull and Bones to ever oppose each other in a presidential race."

Steven continued the story. "Our group started forty-eight years ago. It was founded by Jonathan Wilder, who was a billionaire several times over. He was an industrialist who made his original fortune in commodities, mainly copper, platinum, oil, and gas. When the tech industry started to explode, he became one of the largest chip manufacturers in the industry. He held over 1,100 patents, and almost every tech company in America and some in Europe are connected to him by license.

"He wanted to give back to exceptionally smart individuals in industry and school, so he formed this society, which has grown to what it is today. As of now, there is only one group. It is ours. With a total membership of 410, today we have 268 active members. The rest either have passed on or are retired. Although retired, many of them are still active in the society and will give us counsel if we need it."

"You speak of Wilder in the past tense. Am I to assume he is no longer with us?" Michael asked in a curious tone.

"He passed away twelve years ago at the age of ninety-three. He was a great man," Steven answered sadly. "However, his legacy lives on. His estate was set up to award a perpetual endowment to the society, which we receive each year. The money continues to fund a secret scholarship trust he established for students who excel in business studies. Those who are awarded the scholarship have no idea where the money comes from. Our society secretly pays their tuition and school expenses. To be perfectly honest with you both, and only because we are accepting you as members of Samson and Delilah, I can tell you that you have both been the recipients of Jonathan's generosity. You have no financial worries about your educational expenses right through your PhD or JD studies, if you wish to pursue them."

The boys were stunned by this revelation. Michael asked, "Why were we chosen? I am sure there are a lot smarter students in the world than us."

Ian fielded this question. "It's not only academics. There are other factors that we take into consideration, such as family history, your quest for knowledge in other areas, and so on. Just because someone is book smart doesn't make him a good candidate. We look for a well-rounded person who can help us fulfill our mission. There is so much more than academics involved. As time goes on, you'll understand why you have been chosen."

He didn't want to give away too much at this first encounter, so he ended it there. "For now, I think that's enough. I am sure you have a lot to digest. Speaking of digesting, if you don't have any pressing questions, why don't we end it here and rejoin for dinner."

"That sounds fine with me," Michael said.

"I'm good with that. It has been a long day," Amir added.

"Good, we can continue over dinner," Ian said, as he took out two envelopes and passed them across the table to them. "These are the keys to your rooms at the hotel. You have adjoining suites. There is no need to check in. It has already been taken care of; you can go straight to your rooms.

"There is a driver waiting downstairs to take you to the hotel. His name is Frank. He will be available to take you to the restaurant this evening, and anywhere else you would like to go during your stay with us. We have a 7:30 reservation. If you need anything at the hotel, just sign for it."

With that, Steven opened the curtains in the room and said, "Why don't you take one more look before you go. We'll see you at the restaurant. Your driver knows where to go. By the way, jacket and tie."

The boys took one long look out at the harbor, shook hands with Ian and Steven, and took the elevator to meet their driver.

Their driver was waiting for them. He was about six feet tall, medium build, wearing a black suit, white shirt, and black tie. He did not wear a cap. "You must be Frank," Amir said.

"Then you must be Michael and Amir. Glad to meet you."

"Thank you, Frank. We're glad to be here. I'm Michael, and this is Amir," Michael said, so that Frank would know which of them was which.

Frank took their bags, placed them into the trunk, and held open the door for them. When they entered the black Cadillac limousine, they could smell the rich scent of the new black leather seats as the door closed with a solid thud. It smelled like a new pair of shoes. They could feel the cleanliness of the car like it had just been cleaned.

When they reached the hotel, Frank once again opened the doors for them as the bellman removed their bags from the trunk. Exiting the limo, they immediately noticed the signature sidewalk clock that marked the Sherry Netherland's entrance opposite the south main entrance to Central Park. The hotel had added a note of drama and history to New York City ever since opening in 1927. World leaders and renowned kings and queens had graced its rooms.

Frank said to the bellman, "This is Mr. Ahren and Mr. Haman. They should already be registered."

"Welcome. My name is Howard. We have been expecting you. Let's get you settled in," he said politely. He was wearing a black morning suit tailcoat and grey-striped slacks. A black-and-grey-striped, wide ascot-style tie adorned his wing-tipped collared shirt.

Frank handed Amir his business card and said, "This is my cell number. Whenever you're ready, just call me. I will be less than ten minutes away at any time. I will see you at 7:15 to take you to dinner. The restaurant is only about six minutes from your hotel."

"Thank you," they said in unison. "See you then."

CHAPTER 20

When they entered the lobby through the revolving doors, they found themselves in awe of the décor. The lobby walls were a light marble that showed the luster of over 100 years of polishing. The Gothic arched ceilings were painted in a faux Venetian plaster finish. There was a large crystal fixture hanging from top of the arch in the ceiling. Its polished crystals reflected the eighteen candelabra bulbs that illuminated the lobby. The lobby in front of the registration desk seemed sparse, with only a plush gold sofa, two armchairs, and a side table and lamp resting on the European-style carpet that graced the floor.

Howard escorted them to the elevator and entered the car after them. They were surprised to find an attendant still operating the elevator. When they arrived on the 23rd floor, they were shown to their rooms. "I believe you already have your keys," he said, waiting for confirmation.

Michael handed Howard his key card. Howard placed it in the door slot and opened the door to what might have been the largest hotel room Michael had ever occupied. "After you, Mr. Haman. Let me get you settled first." He walked to the window and opened the gold window curtains, which revealed a magnificent view of Central Park.

It was a breathtaking view, and Michael's eyes opened wide. He laughingly said, "Wow! This sure isn't Kansas."

Howard quickly explained the workings of the temperature controls and light switches in the room. "Mr. Ahren, your room is right next door and is identical. Let me get you settled in. Then you gentlemen are on your own. There is a mini-bar under the desk in each room. Help yourself to anything you desire."

As the bellman, Howard, was about to leave, Michael said, "Thank you, Howard," and tried to tip him with a $5 bill.

"Thank you, but I must refuse. Everything has been taken care of," he said.

After showering and dressing, Michael and Amir went to the lobby of the hotel to meet their driver. They were chauffeured to Daniel's Restaurant, on East 60th Street, for their 7:30 dinner appointment. Once inside, they were escorted to a round table in a very private rear corner of the restaurant. They noticed that the table had five place settings and five chairs. Ian Sellers and Steven Moslek were already seated. Wondering who else was coming to dinner, Amir asked, "From the looks of the settings on this table, it appears we are expecting more company?"

"Yes! We will be joined by one more guest, who couldn't make our meeting this afternoon," Steven answered to remove the puzzled look from Amir's face. "We are being joined by John Malcolm, the CEO of Car Tech, the largest auto group in North America and the current director of the society. He wants to meet both of you personally." His voice was restrained. He spoke with caution in case anyone in the room was within earshot.

"I'm impressed and flattered," Michael said with excitement in his voice.

Just then the hostess escorted John Malcom to their table. Michael and Amir stood up immediately as John approached and introduced himself to them. They shook his hand, and both expressed how honored they were to meet him.

"No, it's my honor," John said humbly. "I have heard a lot about both of you and can't wait for you to join our family." Turning to Steve and Ian, John asked, "Have you filled them in on what's expected of them in the future?"

"Not completely. I thought we would do it over dinner," Ian said.

"Sounds mysterious," Amir said.

"Not really," said John. His voice became lower, and they strained to hear him. "It's really very simple. What we want you to do is finish your degree and continue with your education in graduate school. Get your MBAs and just go with the flow of the society. We will handle the rest. Which includes making sure you get into the school you want. We will cover all your costs including tuition, books, and other expenses. If you want to go on to post-graduate school such as in law, or get your doctorate, that will be covered as well. All we will ask of you when we help you in your career choice is that you pay it forward. We may come to you from time to time with a problem that needs to be solved or a favor that needs attention. We would only ask that you help us with what we need. It's that simple. Everything is aboveboard and completely legal. We don't break any laws, and our integrity is unquestionable. We got you this far; let us take you the rest of the way."

"What do you mean you got us this far?" Michael asked with some ire.

Noticing he seemed a bit angry, John asked, "Did you ever stop and think why it was so easy for you two to get accepted at Wharton? It wasn't just your good grades or good looks. We were pulling some strings behind your backs." Then he spoke to Amir. "Remember that economics class you wanted to take but were told it was closed. Who do you think opened it up for you? We can get things done that you can't imagine. When it comes to your career choices after completing school, all you have to do is tell us where you want to work and in what capacity, and it will be done. Our members have the ability to do almost anything as long as it's legal. Down the road, we would expect the same from you. No questions asked. You will be given an assignment, and you will carry it out to the best of your ability. That's all we ask in return."

"What if I don't want to join your society? Not that I'm saying no," Michael put in.

"No problem—you finish school, get your bachelor's degree, and we part friends. After that you are on your own. We never met, there is no society, and that's that. We just consider it an investment that didn't go the way we hoped. We are not that callous that we would hurt you in any way. But we certainly want our investment to pay off. So we hope you will join us."

As the server came over to take their order, the conversation became muted. When the server left. Amir turned to Michael and asked, "You aren't having second thoughts, are you?"

"No, not at all. I was just playing devil's advocate."

"It's understandable. We expect you to have some doubts. Most people would. On the other hand, we hope you accept our offer," John said.

"Well, to be honest with you, Amir and I have discussed it, and we would love to, as you put it so admirably, join your family."

"That's wonderful. I can speak for all three of us," John said motioning with his hand to acknowledge Ian and Steven, "and say welcome. You will never regret your decision."

"Where do we go from here?" asked Amir.

"It's simple. You go back to school and finish your studies. We know you want to go on to graduate school and get your MBAs. Have you given any thought to remaining at Wharton, or would you like to continue somewhere else? You just tell us where, and it will be done. But you don't have to make that decision for a few months, so don't even worry about it now."

"No! I think I can speak for both of us," Amir said. "Michael and I had previously discussed grad school, and we would like to continue at Wharton, where we feel comfortable. We know the professors and campus, and it would be an easy transition for us, so why upset the apple cart?"

Michael nodded in agreement.

"Then consider it done. Make out your applications and send them to me. We will take care of the rest. And by the way, let's find a nice two-bedroom apartment for both of you off campus. I understand the dorms there are a little cramped."

"To say the least! I always wondered how they got sardines in a can. Now I know; send them to college," Michael said with a hearty chuckle.

They all laughed. Meanwhile, the server was placing their appetizers on the table. "Let's eat," Ian interjected.

For the next hour and a half, they finished their dinners, devouring the French entrées that Daniel's was known for. Michael had duck à l'orange with wild rice and creamed spinach, while Amir dinned on pecan-crusted sea bass with mashed potatoes and asparagus. When they finished dessert, they said good-bye and left for the evening, each going in his own direction. Michael and Amir met their driver and were chauffeured back to the hotel.

They retired for the evening and traveled back to Philadelphia the next morning.

During the next semester, Michael and Amir continued their studies and continued attending society meetings monthly. Most meetings were routine, with those present giving opinions on recent corporate decisions in various industries and what they would mean to their businesses and shareholders. At one particular meeting, it was announced that Ian Sellers was being promoted to CEO of Verizon. It was also announced that John Malcom's term as president of the society was expiring, and he would be succeed by Sellers.

During another meeting it was announced there were going to be several corporate takeovers within the next six months. These mergers and acquisitions would change the face of the corporate world forever. When all these consolidations were completed, there would be fewer companies to do business with within any particular industry. It appeared no industry was safe—transportation, telecommunications, food, energy, and logistics, to begin with.

Amir and Michael finished their studies and went on to graduate with a perfect grade-point index of 4.0. The following semester they started graduate school. Two years later they graduated with their MBAs in hand, with top honors.

There was nothing to do after graduation except take some time off and get ready for the job market.

A week after graduation, they attended the last meeting of the Samson and Delilah Society before the summer break. Ian Sellers asked the boys, "Have you given any thought to what you want to do this summer during your break?"

"I haven't given it much thought," Michael answered.

Amir echoed the same.

"How would you boys like to cruise the Mediterranean and Greek Isles while working on a little project for us? Of course all your expenses will be paid by us," he added. "You don't have to answer me now. You can take your time to think it over." He originally had not been going to ask them at this meeting but thought it might be necessary to take their thoughts off this evening's topic, which had seemed to invade their minds.

"What's there to think about?" Amir said. "Count me in."

"What am I, chopped liver?" Michael added. "I'm on board. When do we set sail?"

"In ten days. You will be gone for about five to six weeks. There will be some paperwork for you to do, and some business plans we want you to help us explore. Other than that, not much else. There will be plenty of time for fun and sun; I promise you."

CHAPTER 21

It was going to be a glorious vacation. After they completed their first class flight from New York's JFK Airport to Athens, Greece, Michael and Amir were picked up at the airport by a limousine for the thirty-minute ride to the pier, where they were to board the yacht belonging to Ian's company.

The ride took them through the city, where traffic was unusually heavy. The inside of the limousine smelled like beer. The driver apologized, explaining that the last passenger had spilled a bottle of beer on his ride. "Last rider drunk, spilled beer. I not have time to clean car," he said in broken English with a heavy Greek accent.

As they entered the waterfront, the driver pointed to a yacht. "Your ship," he said.

Upon seeing the yacht for the first time, the boys were flabbergasted. They exited the car quickly, trying to leave the smell of the brew behind. As the driver removed their bags from the trunk and placed them on the dock, the boys just stood there, admiring the yacht.

The smell of the beer was quickly banished by the aroma of the salt air, which was filled with the sounds of seagulls squealing through the air as they searched for scraps of fish that were floating in the water from fishing boats that had cleaned their catches.

They couldn't believe their eyes. "Holy shit," Michael exclaimed. "Look at that damn boat!"

"I see it, and I can't believe what I am looking at. That has to be the largest private boat I ever saw," Amir added.

The 310-foot-long custom-built mega yacht that would carry them away across the calm waters of the Mediterranean had three decks encased in black one-way glass. Above the top deck, amidships, was the bridge, which took up about twenty percent of the surface of the deck below it. The yacht's sleek, black hull with broad gold pin-striping was gleaming in the bright sun. Its decks were teak, decorated with the finest comforts. If it weren't for its size, it would have looked more like a sporty race car than a yacht. On the third deck aft was a bare platform, which was a landing pad for a helicopter. Although they didn't know it at the time, all the glass on the ship was bulletproof.

Two deck hands suspended on boatswain chairs were on the side of the yacht, washing the hull with large sponge mops. Another ship's mate was polishing the brass rails of the upper deck. On the bow, painted in bold gold letters, was the name of the yacht, "Ma Bell," which had been the nickname for the phone company when it had all been part of AT&T. The name also appeared on the stern.

"Don't call it a boat. It's a ship. A boat is what you look for when a ship starts to sink," a voice from behind them said with a laugh. The boys turned to see a tall, six-foot, well-tanned man in a captain's uniform walking toward them. He had dark hair and brown eyes and was slender for his height. He extended his hand to them and said, "I am Captain Peter Wellington. You must be Amir and Michael, my passengers for the next few weeks."

"That's us," Amir answered. "Sorry about the boat comment."

They shook hands and laughed as they exchanged pleasantries. "Let's go on board and get started. Don't worry about your bags—we'll take care of them," Captain Wellington said as he guided the boys up the gangway. Two ship's mates followed behind with their luggage.

They were met by two stewardesses, who introduced themselves as Jennifer and Shari. They were dressed in navy blue skirts and white blouses. Red silk scarves, tied to the side, adorned their necks. Their feet were covered in white two-inch pumps, which accented their tan legs. Both women were tall, in their late twenties, and very attractive.

Jennifer was tall and slender, five feet nine inches, weighing about 130 pounds, with green eyes and long blonde hair that draped the sides of her face and rested on her shoulders. Shari was five feet seven inches, about 120 pounds. She had long brown hair secured in a ponytail and blue eyes that seemed to pierce right through you. Both women had olive complexions. It was hard to tell if it was from exposure to the sun or their heritage. They could have passed for sisters.

"We will be your attendants during your stay with us," Jennifer said. "Anything you need, just ask. If it's on board, it's yours. If it's not, we'll get it for you. Can I offer you a drink? Unfortunately there are no alcoholic beverages on board, so juice, water, or soft drinks will have to do."

"Water is fine with me," Michael said. "We don't drink alcohol."

"I'm fine with water," Amir echoed.

Reaching into a cooler next to the railing, she retrieved two bottles of water and handed them to the boys.

"Let me show you to your cabins. I am sure you want to freshen up after your long flight." As they walked to their cabins. Jennifer explained, "The ship carries a crew of twenty-eight. There is Captain Wellington, whom you already met, his first officer, Lester, whom you will meet later, a navigator, an executive and sous chef, a chief mechanic, two assistants, eleven service people including three cabin stewards, seven deck hands, and of course Shari and myself." They rode a glass-enclosed elevator, which looked out over the seaport, to the middle deck.

Jennifer handed Michael and Amir key cards to their suites. "The captain is going to set sail for Santorini, which will be our first port. Your luggage should already be in your cabins. When you are ready, just pick up the telephone and dial #72. We will come to get you and show you around. We'll see you whenever you're ready."

When they opened their cabin doors, they saw that the rooms were identical. The boys couldn't believe their accommodations. Each suite was about 1200 square feet. They each contained a king-size bed, a dresser, and night stands, and a walk-in closet. There was an alcove with a large mahogany desk, a leather desk chair, a leather recliner with an ottoman, and a full-size leather sofa. On each desk was a laptop computer with an array of pencils, pens and writing tablets. A one-way glass sliding door opened from the office alcove to a large balcony. A sixty-inch flat screen TV with a complete surround sound system was built into the wall in front of the bed. A smaller, forty-two-inch TV was attached to the wall in the alcove.

The bathroom contained a white marble, glass-enclosed stall shower with five shower heads, a full Jacuzzi tub, and two marble sinks. Besides the toilet there was a bidet for female passengers. Michael almost gasped when he looked around his suite. *Wow! I feel like I'm in heaven. These guys really know how to live,* he thought to himself. Both boys quickly settled in, unpacked, and showered. About an hour later, Amir knocked on Michael's door and said, "I'm ready for the tour. What about you?"

"I can't wait to see what the rest of this ship looks like. Could you believe these rooms? I thought the ones we had in New York were huge." He answered his own question rhetorically. Then he pick up the phone and dialed Jennifer.

"Just take the elevator up to level three. We'll be waiting for you there to show you around."

They were met by both women, who handed each of them a glass of iced tea with an orange slice in it. "Thank you," they said simultaneously. When they looked around the room, which was about forty by sixty feet in size, they couldn't help but notice the furnishings. It contained two large, three-sided white leather sofas, which were set up as conversation pits in one third of the room. An oval-shaped black marble bar and twelve stools were positioned between the sofas. The bar could be accessed from either side.

On the far side of the room was a regulation size billiards table. Two games tables, each with six leather arm chairs were on the other side of the room. There were two seventy-two-inch flat screen TVs on each side, which could be viewed from anywhere in the room. On the walls that didn't contain TVs there were original works of art. They easily recognized the Chagalls, Picassos, Monets and Miros that were perfectly hung so they would be obvious to anyone entering the room. Also hanging on the walls were several glass sculptures by Chihuly.

"This is our recreation room. It contains just about anything you need to entertain yourself. Through those doors you'll find a library that contains over 1,500 books of almost every genre. It also contains a conference room table used for corporate meetings." Shari said, as she pointed to a pair of glass French doors at the far side of the room. "Let's tour the rest of the ship. After that I'll introduce you to the chef, who will prepare a light snack for you before dinner." They toured each deck and were astonished at the décor.

Later they snacked on hors d'oeuvres of sushi, crab cakes, and baked brie with raspberries prepared by the executive chef, whom they were introduced to as Chris. "If you get hungry late at night and would like a snack, just pick up the phone and dial the galley. Whatever you want will be delivered to your suite in a few minutes."

Their tour lasted about one hour and took them from one end of the ship to the other, ending on the bridge with the captain and first officer. After that they were ready for dinner.

They proceeded to the dining room, on the middle deck, not far from their cabins. Both sides of the room's walls were constructed of panels of one-way glass, which allowed them to look out without anyone being able to look in. They were seated at a rosewood dining table with twenty-four chairs. Chris served them, assisted by both stewardesses. They ate a four-course meal, consisting of a Greek salad, followed by orzo soup, then a rack of rosemary and garlic lamb chops, with mashed potatoes, and green peas sautéed in tomato sauce with thyme.

"I hope you enjoy your meal," Chris said after serving the entrée. "After all, we are in Greece." Their entrées were followed by a dessert of sweet baklava, an assortment of powdered sugar-coated lemon cookies, and strong Greek coffee.

After dinner they wandered up to the entertainment center and played a few games of backgammon until they found themselves dozing at the game table. It seemed the long day and jet lag had gotten the best of them. They found themselves in bed before ten.

CHAPTER 22

The next morning, Michael and Amir awoke to find the ship docked in Santorini. They felt well rested as they made their way to the dining room. They were joined by Captain Wellington, who was already seated at the table, for a hearty breakfast. As they sat at the dining room table, they were overcome with the sweet smell of the cinnamon French toast, pancakes, and sweet rolls, which were arrayed on a serving cart next to the table; the smell of fresh-brewed coffee washed the air. Enough silverware for a four-course meal, a crystal water glass, and a white porcelain dinner plate and cup and saucer, framed by blue woven place mats, were set for three people. There was a bread plate with a butter knife to the left of the place mat.

Captain Wellington, putting down his coffee cup, said to the boys as they were taking their seats, "Good morning. I hope you had a good first night. Has either of you boys ever been to Santorini?"

"No," they both answered.

"Well, let me tell you what our day here will be like. This morning we have arranged for a local tour guide, who will show you around all day. You can come back to the ship for lunch, which would take up considerable time, or eat at a local restaurant, which I suggest. That way you can get a taste of the local cuisine. Dinner will be served at seven, so judge your time accordingly."

Captain Wellington placed two walkie-talkies on the table. "These will help you reach the ship if you need to call for anything. They have two channels. Channel one is to talk between each other if you get separated. Channel two will reach the bridge if you need anything. I have to leave and attend to some matters with the ship. Enjoy your breakfast, and have a great day. I will see you for dinner."

The boys left the ship to be greeted by an attractive, young, local tour guide named Patricia Ann, who was waiting at the bottom of the gangway. About five feet six inches tall and around 115 pounds, she had brown eyes and light brown, medium-length straight hair. She was wearing a yellow cotton dress and white canvas tennis shoes. After introducing herself, she asked the boys to call her Patsy. She spoke perfect English, explaining that she had studied in England for two years.

They proceeded up the concrete pier, passing souvenir shops along the way, to a funicular, about 100 yards away. The car, which had room for four people, took them to the top of the cliff by themselves to visit the village. On the ride up, they noticed tourists who'd decided to ride the donkeys up the steep cliffs steps to the top. Amir turned to Michael and said, "The last thing I want to do is ride a smelly donkey on a hot day like today." They all laughed.

Patsy explained some of the history of the island. "Santorini is 980 feet high, surrounded by steep cliffs on three sides. It is what remained after a massive volcanic eruption that destroyed the earliest settlements. It was once a single island. The volcano's eruption created a giant rectangular lagoon and a smaller island named Theresia, which is located on the fourth side of Santorini, between the lagoon and the sea. The lagoon is connected to the sea on two sides. The depth of the caldera, created by the volcano's eruption, is over 1,200 feet deep. That's what makes it possible for most of the large ships to anchor anywhere in the bay. There are over 15,000 people living on the island, which measures about 28 square miles."

Both Michael and Amir were impressed with these facts, which seemed to roll off her tongue. "I bet you tell that story a lot," Amir said.

"Almost every day," she answered with a smile. "I can tell it in my sleep." She laughed.

Just then their ride ended. When they exited the cable car they couldn't help noticing the design of the village. The buildings were glaring white with blue trim. Except for the bright blue domes of the churches, the roofs of the buildings were also white stucco. The reflection from the architectural finishes was almost blinding. The view of the Aegean Sea from the top of the cliff was breathtaking. The sun presented the azure color of the water to them like the sparkle of a blue sapphire.

They spent the day sightseeing and visiting local merchants' shops, pushing their way through the throngs of visiting tourists from cruise ships that were docked in the area. Patsy guided them around town, showing them local art galleries, jewelry stores, and souvenir shops. At one shop, Michael purchased some local postcards, which he wanted to send to his mother, whom he missed dearly.

When it was time for lunch, they ate at a local gyro restaurant, where they quickly wolfed down the combination lamb, beef, and salad wrapped in pita bread. Amir said, "I can't believe I was so ravenous after that breakfast we ate. I guess all this sightseeing and walking makes you hungry."

They returned to the ship about 5:30, fatigued and hungry once again. They knew they would sleep well this night. Patsy waved good-bye to them as they walked up the gangway.

After dinner they returned to their suites early to escape the exhaustion of the day. The next day was a repeat of the day before, except that this time they were docked in Mykonos.

After Mykonos, they cruised to Rhodes, and then onto Euboea, the largest of the Greek Islands, where they spent the day at a local beach and swam in the Aegean Sea.

CHAPTER 23

That evening Captain Wellington charted a course to Istanbul, Turkey. At dinner he told the boys that it was about 275 nautical miles from their present location. "We should be there by morning," he stated.

Once they had cleared customs and were able to go ashore, they were once again joined by a local guide, who led them through the city. Mehmet was a young man in his late twenties, of Turkish descent, who understood English well, as with most Turkish people.

Their first stop was the Grand Bazaar, where they spent hours moving from merchant to merchant. Its shops are located in a cavernous underground market, which is more like a giant cave than a shopping mall. It would have taken them weeks to visit each shop. As they moved from stall to stall, they realized it wouldn't be hard to get lost walking through the immense number of corridors lined with every shop imaginable. Michael said to Amir, "No matter what happens, don't lose sight of Mehmet, or we'll never get home." They both laughed.

Sometime into their third hour at the bazaar, Michael looked at Amir. "I don't know about you, but I've had enough shopping. If I never see another

Turkish carpet, evil eye or cashmere scarf in my life, I won't be sad," he said with a big grin. Amir and Mehmet both laughed along with him.

They left the bazaar and walked about twenty minutes to the Süleymaniye Mosque, known as the Blue Mosque. "It was built in 1550, on the order of Sultan Süleyman," Mehmet told them. "It took three years to complete and stands as the largest mosque in Turkey. It is a combination of Islamic and Byzantine architecture. It was ravaged in a fire in 1660 and was restored. Its giant dome collapsed during an earthquake in 1776 and was restored once again. During WWII, its courtyard was used as an ammunition depot, which caught fire and damaged it once more. It was refurbished for the last time in 1956. The original color of the dome ceiling was blue. That is why they call it the 'Blue Mosque.' Today the dome is redder."

Michael suddenly felt excited. The cascading dome and six tall minarets were overpowering. They dominated the skyline of Istanbul. He had studied about it and seen pictures of it as a child in Indonesia, but he'd never thought he would ever see it in person. He was overwhelmed by its immense size and towering dome. When the call to prayer echoed from its towers halfway through their day, he felt a nervousness and emotional movement inside of him he could not explain. He had not prayed the Qur'an in many years, since returning to the U.S. with his mother.

They visited Topkapi Palace, where they viewed the royal jewels. Amir tried sneaking a forbidden picture of the Topkapi Diamond, to the chagrin of a palace guard, who admonished him by tapping him on the shoulder and waggling his finger at him from side to side, indicating it was forbidden.

At the spice market they were overwhelmed by the magnificent colors of all the spices and Turkish delights, from jellies, dried fruits, and nuts to halvah and licorice candies, all of which were displayed. The pungent aroma of the spices filled their nostrils. It reminded Michael of when he would help his mother prepare meals. He remembered assisting her in the kitchen as a young boy. He would sniff each jar of spice she was using, some irritating his nose, sometimes making him sneeze.

When they were ready to leave the market, Mehmet said he would get them a taxi back to the pier. When he hailed a cab, he spoke to the driver in Turkish and told him where to take the boys. "It's a short ride to the boat. Don't give the driver any more than ten dollars," Mehmet told them.

"Thank you, Mehmet. Thanks for a great day," Michael said.

When they entered the taxi, they were immediately overcome by the awful smell of tobacco. The seats and headliner were soaked with cigarette smoke that was almost nauseating. And, to add insult to injury, the driver had a lit, unfiltered cigarette dangling from his lips, which only added to the vile stench. The car was old and hot, without air-conditioning. It rattled on the narrow cobblestone streets and sounded at times like the wheels would fall off. Michael and Amir sat with their faces out the open windows, trying to get some fresh air. They didn't know which was worse: the secondhand smoke or the outside pollution. They couldn't wait for the ride to end.

When the taxi arrived at the pier, Amir handed the driver a ten-dollar bill and quickly left the car. Michael was already out the other door, practically gasping for air. They looked at each other and nervously laughed.

As they turned towards the *Ma Bell*, the first thing they noticed was a black, Bell Jet Ranger helicopter perched on the landing pad. Looking at each other, Michael said curiously, "I wonder what that's all about."

"There's only one way to find out. Let's get on board."

When they were at the end of the gangway, they were met by Jennifer. "Why don't you go to your suites, freshen up, and get ready for dinner, and we'll meet on the recreation deck at seven o'clock."

Amir looked at his watch. It was 5:40.

Michael asked, "What's with the helicopter?"

"We have visitors this evening, who will be joining us for dinner. You will see them at seven."

Both boys rode the elevator to their suites, showered, and changed for dinner. It was 6:58 when they appeared on the appointed deck, right on time.

As they stepped off the elevator into the dining room, Michael immediately saw Ian Sellers, who was standing with another man he didn't recognize. As he walked over to shake hands and greet him,

Michael seemed dumbfounded as he witnessed Amir briskly walk over to the other man, put his arms around him in a tight hug, kiss him on the cheek, and exclaim, "Dad, I didn't know you were going to be here."

"Wait a minute. This is your father?" Michael asked, shocked by Amir's declaration.

"Yes! Michael, say hello to my father, Leon Ahren."

As Michael greeted him with a firm handshake, he said, "It's a pleasure to finally meet you, sir. I thought you were traveling. What brings you here?"

"Many things. Actually I am going to be part of a meeting we will be conducting tomorrow. We may be joined by others via a teleconference, but for the time being it will start off with the four of us. I hate to be the bearer of unpleasant news, but it seems we will be interrupting your vacation for a few days."

"Don't feel bad about it. After all the sightseeing we have done the past few days, I could use the rest," Amir said.

"Well, that might be fine for your body, but we may tax your mind. Let's have dinner," he said with authority in his voice. Michael thought to himself that it might be Amir's father who would be conducting this meeting.

They proceeded to the dining room deck and spent the next two hours talking about what the boys had been doing while vacationing, politics, books, art, and any other topic that would take them afar from the real purpose of their being aboard. Michael got the feeling that the purpose for this assembly was being intentionally avoided. He felt mystified at why they seemed to be obscuring the real reason for being here.

At one point in the conversation, Michael asked of Leon, "What is it you do?"

"I am an economist. I crunch numbers for a living."

Somehow, Michael believed there was more to his answer than just a being a numbers cruncher. He knew his place, though, so he didn't pursue it further.

As they were getting up from the dinner table, Leon turned to his son and said, "I am taking a walk on the deck. Why don't you join me so we can catch up? I haven't seen you in months."

"Sure, Dad. Why not!"

"You guys go ahead; I am sure you have much to talk about. I'll see you in the morning," As he turned to leave the dining room, Michael asked, "What time is breakfast?"

"Nine," Ian answered. "See you in the morning. Good night, Michael."

CHAPTER 24

A s they walked the deck, Leon and Amir made small talk for a few minutes. They talked about family, school, and all the pleasant things parents talk about to their children when they haven't seen them for a while. As they approached a group of deck chairs, Leon said to his son, "Sit. Let's talk." The two men each sat down on the side of a chair, facing each other, their knees almost touching.

"How are you and Michael getting along? Do you have any difficulties between you?"

"What do you mean by difficulties?"

"I guess what I am asking is whether you basically agree with each other on politics and the world situation."

"Absolutely! Let me tell you about Michael. I know you just met him for the first time, and you only know about him from what I have told you over the years and the intelligence your office has gathered. So I want you to know this: We are like one person. We think alike, enjoy the same books and movies…it's hard for us to disagree. We even finish each other's sentences at times. Michael and I are so close that if I could chose anyone in the world to have as a brother it would be him. Dad, I know that if we were ever in a situation that called for drastic action, Michael would take a bullet for me, and I would for him."

"I'm not surprised by your statement. It reflects what you've told me about him in your phone calls and e-mails. I wish I could say that about some of the people I have become friends with."

"Dad, you can't believe the trust and confidence we have in each other."

"I'm glad to hear that because I'm about to ask something of you that might test that trust."

Amir's mind started to become cloudy. He believed he knew what was coming next from his father but was afraid to face it.

"Amir, how much does Michael know about the society and the project?"

"Not much at all. He knows about the society's influence on business and political leaders."

Leon Ahren continued, "Here is our current problem: It's time to tell Michael the truth. And you must be the one to tell him."

"Why me?"

"Because he trusts you, and from what I know of your relationship, he believes in you. It has to come from you. He knows us in the society for less than three years; he knows you for over six. That says a lot about a relationship. He knows me for only a few hours. All I can do is show him the evidence that will corroborate what you tell him, but you have to convince him to listen to it. I know you can do this, Amir. I have much confidence in you. Make me proud of you once again."

"When do you want me to talk to him?"

"As soon as possible. Tomorrow after breakfast. This way we can fill him in with the details in the afternoon."

"All right, Dad, but don't for one minute believe I am going to get a good night's sleep."

Both men stood up to leave, Leon giving his son a tight hug. The father pressed his cheek to his son's and whispered in his ear, "I know this will be difficult for you, Amir, but it must be done." He then kissed him on the cheek.

"I know. Good night, Father," he said as he turned and walked away to return to his cabin.

Leon Ahren stood at the rail looking out at the water. The lights from the opposite shore seemed to be dancing on the water between the European and Asian divide of Istanbul. He felt troubled because of the position he had put his son in. However, he knew it had to be done. The free world depended on it.

CHAPTER 25

When they awoke the next morning, they were cruising at sea.

All throughout breakfast, Amir's stomach was doing flip-flops, as though he had just come off a wild rollercoaster ride and knew that he was about to give back his earlier meal. He was fearful he wouldn't be able to keep his food down. He had played this scenario over in his mind as he tossed and turned, not being able to sleep. All night he'd been fighting with his pillow as well as with his conscience. He knew when he came down for breakfast that the task ahead of him was daunting, but it had to be done, and he was the person who had to do it. He barely ate.

"Wow, for a person with a usually monstrous appetite, you haven't touched your breakfast. Are you all right?" Michael asked.

"I'm fine, just not that hungry. I wasn't feeling well last night. I'm going up on the deck for some air. Why don't you meet me there after you finish? We need to talk about a few things."

"Sure!" Michael's curiosity level was rising as he realized that Amir sounded troubled. He hurriedly finished, excused himself, and left to meet his friend.

"Okay, I'm here. What's up?"

"Sit down. I have to tell you an unbelievable story, and I don't know how you're going to take it. I'm asking you not to judge what I'm about to tell you until I finish. I'm asking you to put all your trust in what you are about to learn, and I can only assure you that what you are about to hear is the absolute truth. And, there is nothing you or I can do to change it."

"Amir, you're really frightening me. I am...."

Amir cut him off mid-sentence. "Just listen, please, before I lose my courage."

Michael became frightened. He didn't know what to expect. Amir started to speak again.

"The first thing I must tell you is that what you are about to learn is enormously confidential. Not a word of this can leak out. The entire free world depends on our secrecy."

"I promise, but what the hell are you talking about—'the entire free world'?"

"Michael, please just listen." Amir was getting anxious and frustrated. "I am not who you think I am. Don't get me wrong—my real name is Amir Ahren. But I am not a Moslem. I am a Jew. My name, although it sounds Arabic, is really Hebrew. I am an Israeli pretending to be a Moslem for reasons that you will soon understand. I am your best friend. I would do anything for you and would never intentionally do you harm. No, I am not gay, and I don't possess any supernatural powers." He believed a little light humor might help to calm down his nerves.

Michael laughed a little but was still quite confused. He was becoming agitated and angry that his best friend might have deceived him all these years. But for what reason, he wondered.

"Get on with it. The suspense is killing me. If you've got something to say, just spit it out." He spoke emphatically.

"All right, let me start with my father. Let me tell you a little about him. He is an economist—or, as he put it, he crunches numbers for a living. It's a little deeper than that. My father is with the Israeli Government. His title is "minister of finance." It would be equivalent to the secretary of the treasury in the U.S."

"I don't understand. Why would…."

Amir cut him off again. "Please, Michael, no questions yet. This is hard enough for me."

Michael sensed he was very distraught. "Okay, I won't say a word." He had so many questions at this point, and Amir had only begun. Michael was projecting his feelings although he hadn't heard the entire story.

Amir went on. "About thirty-five-years ago, my father, before he was appointed minister of finance, and his staff became aware of an unbelievable plot by a radical Islamic group to literally take over the world. Their intent is to accomplish it without the use of terrorism.

"They are all members of the Samson and Delilah Society and have been planted there over the years by a Middle Eastern Islamic group that is putting an inconceivable plan in place. They are almost there and have the secret support of some extremely high political leaders, who are part of the conspiracy. One of these powerful political leaders is the head of their operation. They must be stopped. Michael, you probably won't believe this, but your life has been taken over by these radicals. You have unknowingly been groomed since you were a child. It started when you were a student in Indonesia at the mosque and continued in America."

"How do you know about my attending a mosque?"

"There is a lot we know, and much more."

Michael couldn't believe what he was hearing. His head was throbbing so much, he felt it was about to explode. He had no idea what to expect next. "What else do you know?"

"Please, Michael, just listen. Did you ever wonder how you were able to attend private elementary and high school on a scholarship? It was all done to keep an eye on you and continue to groom you as you matured."

"This is a sick joke, isn't it? And who is this 'we'?"

"No, unfortunately this is no joke. You must trust me. We have known each other too long and too well for me to joke about this. If you think this is easy for me, you are mistaken. The people who are going to try to stop these madmen from carrying out their plan believed it was time for you to know the truth."

Michael's eyes widened, his heart was pounding, and his breathing became labored. He took a deep breath and exhaled with a heavy sigh. "What else haven't you told me?"

"There is a lot I haven't told you. But my father is going to fill you in later after lunch. He has all the documentation to prove to you that what I have been telling you is real and imminent."

Tears welled up in Amir's eyes. He suddenly felt beyond his years. He was the linchpin in keeping Michael interested and curious enough to face the truth. Michael realized Amir was troubled by what he had just revealed.

"Do you really expect me to eat lunch after what you told me?" He smiled a tense grin and uttered a nervous laugh.

"That is why I couldn't eat breakfast. My father told me last night that I had to tell you the truth, and it had to be today. Please keep an open mind and don't judge us until you hear everything. I know you will be astonished by what you learn."

"What about Ian? Is he part of the conspiracy?"

"No, Ian is not. We are the only members of the society who know what their real mission is; now you know. When you learn everything, hopefully you will understand why we need your help to defeat them."

"I am totally confused. I can't believe you have been living with me in a lie all these years."

"Michael, you have no idea how many times I wanted to tell you the truth. I couldn't. It was and is so vital to our mission to stop them that we couldn't risk any of it." He felt contrite.

"You keep saying 'we,' Amir. Who is 'we'?"

"My father will be able to fill you in with all the answers later. I promise you."

"How can they be stopped if, as you say, they are so powerful?"

"I don't have all the answers. I have not been made aware of all the information. My only mission so far was to gain your trust and confidence in me so I could get you to join us in stopping this madness. I only know that plans have been put in place to destroy their conspiracy. It is a top secret plan that involves many people doing many things who must work together to end this insanity that could destroy the free world as we know it today."

"Mission! I was your mission? Is that what you call me? Your mission. What do you think I am, some piece of real estate that has to be captured or a bridge that has to be blown up?" Michael was angry and shouting. He suddenly felt betrayed and alone.

Amir tried to calm him down. "Michael, please, I didn't want it this way. It is the only way these people can be stopped. You have been unknowingly used like a pawn in a chess game by them. Your life has been guided by outside forces that you have no idea of the dangerousness of."

Michael saw he had tears in his eyes. "Stop crying and act like a man. You expect me to believe this crap? How do I know you are telling me the truth?"

"You don't. Not yet! But there is proof. My father has it and is ready to show it to you. All I ask of you is to trust me and have an open mind. Just listen and make up your own mind. No one is asking you to do anything you don't want to."

"How am I supposed to trust you now after you tell me you have been deceiving me all these years?"

"Because I love you like a brother."

"Brothers don't treat each other this way."

"I am asking you to give me just one chance to prove to you that everything I told you is the truth."

Amir moved closer to hug him. Michael pushed him away. "I want to see your father and all his evidence now; not after lunch," he said with much bitterness and disdain. He turned to walk off the deck. Turning back he said, "I'll be in my cabin. Call me when you are ready, and make it soon. If we weren't at sea, I would be off this ship and you would never see me again." He spoke with hatred in his voice.

"I can understand your feelings. I would probably feel the same way if the tables were turned."

CHAPTER 26

They sat at the conference table in the ship's library. Michael sat in the end chair on one side of the table. Leon Ahren was at the head of the table perpendicular to him, and Ian Sellers was seated two chairs down from Amir, who was opposite Michael. Michael sat there with his arms folded across his chest; his face carried an angry look.

The minister of finance began to speak, "Some of what I am about to show you is highly confidential and top secret. The documents I am about to revel to you are everything we know and you know since you were a young boy in Indonesia. It details every part of your life from that time until today. I am about to reveal to you things that will prove that what I am saying is the absolute truth, and nothing you or I say or do can alter those facts. Some of these things may make you angry, while others may confuse you to the point of disbelief.

Amir has told you things that you may have believed or not. He told you things that I asked him to tell you. He is my son, and although my flesh and blood he has a mission to accomplish. We all have a mission to accomplish. Amir also works for the Israeli government. This is no different than going to war. As I said before, everything contained in the documents I am about to show you is the truth. I need to ask you to keep everything I tell you in complete confidence. Whether you want to believe it or not, the fate of the entire free world is dependent on your promise and secrecy. I know this is a lot to ask of a young man. But I assure you my government, as of now, is the only one with this information, and it must be kept secret. People have actually died protecting this information."

Michael was in shock and remained silent as he looked across the table at Amir, who was focused on Michael's face. Wide eyed, he asked, "You know what's in these papers?"

"Not everything," Amir answered.

"What about you, Ian?'

"Some!"

Leon Ahren continued. "I need to tell you before I proceed that you can change your mind about learning what we know, but once I reveal this information to you it would be hard for you to let go of it. It may cloud your mind. Anytime you want me to stop and take a break, just say so."

Michael's curiosity level was beyond belief. He felt a wave of fear come over him. His mouth was dry. Reaching for a drink of water he said, "Let's proceed."

"Okay! Your parents, Alan and Sylvia, were living in Indonesia, where your father worked for the Ameri-Pro Corporation. Shortly after arriving in Indonesia your mother discovered she was pregnant. They returned to Atlanta, Georgia, so you would be born in America as a natural born citizen, which occurred on June 10, 2008. One month later they returned to Indonesia, where you were raised until you were almost twelve years old. When your father died you returned to Atlanta with your mother. You were an exceptional student in a private grammar and intermediate school. After junior high school, you attended a private high school. All of your education was paid for completely by a scholarship that your mother believed was from the Ameri-Pro Corporation. You lived at home until you went off to college, under another scholarship. This one was from the Samson and Delilah Society. It was there at the Wharton School you met Amir. Is that correct so far?"

"Yes!" Michael felt anxious and wondered what else they knew about him.

Leon Ahren then told Michael everything about his schooling, and the fact that he attended a madrassa in Jakarta and spent time studying Wahhabism. "I know you know the Qur'an from cover to cover and studied it intensely. Until fourteen years ago when you moved back to America, you prayed the Qur'an like a proud Moslem. Your father was not a practicing Moslem, and your mother was Jewish, which under the Talmud makes you Jewish by birth.

I also know you studied some Judaism after you moved back to Atlanta because your mother wanted you to learn of her faith. She wanted you to have some religious identity but didn't force her religion on you. She hoped you would decide for yourself when you matured what you wanted to follow. You never celebrated a bar mitzvah, something your mother hoped you would do. You are proficient in not only the teachings of the Qur'an but the Old Testament as well. You speak fluent Bahasa and are skilled in Arabic and French. Do I have it right so far?"

Michael answered, "Yes! How do you know all this?"

"We know that and much more. Things that you do not know. Things that I am going to reveal to you that you may find hard to believe. But they are true, and I can and will prove every one of them to you. Do you remember this man?" He removed a photo from a folder in front of him and showed it to Michael.

"Yes! That's Arbry Talem." He felt uneasy as he held the black and white photo in his hand starring at it. Suddenly he started to relive his days in Indonesia. He tried to remember when he had seen Arbry for the last time.

"He was your teacher and mentor in Indonesia. His name at that time was Arbry Talem?

He didn't show up for class one day. You were told that he had suddenly moved back to the U.S., and you never saw him again?"

"That's right."

"What if I told you he is alive, and we know exactly where he is and what he is doing? What if I told you he is working high up in the U.S. government and has a new name and new identity?"

"How can that be?

"It is so, Michael. He is a traitor and is leading a plan that will change the face of the world forever. It's true. He was groomed to be where he is. A radical imam at a mosque in Chicago, where he originally came from, believed that he was more impressionable and easier to convince to follow radical Islam than anyone else. He is a Harvard undergraduate and a Harvard Law School graduate. He became the chosen one. He was sent to Indonesia to study Wahhabism. He was then sent to the mosque where you were studying to become your mentor and teacher. He spent a year abroad after completing his undergraduate degree, before going on to law school. His task was to befriend you and convert you to radical Islam. The imam at your mosque believed that you were smarter and more open to suggestion than he was, only you were too young. You were just a young boy. They didn't have the time to wait for you to grow up to carry out their plans."

"I don't believe it."

"Michael, you have no idea how powerful and how much influence these people have." Leon Ahren was troubled at what he was about to reveal. He wasn't sure how Michael would accept what he was about to tell him. But he had no other choice.

"This is may be difficult for you to believe. Your father died before your twelfth birthday. Your mother and you were told it was a work-related accident. That is not true. Your father was murdered," he said emphatically.

"I don't believe that either," Michael said with anger in his voice.

"It is true. We captured the person who committed that horrendous act. He set it up to look like an accident. He spent nine years in an Israeli prison until he died of a brain tumor while he was imprisoned. However, before he died he recorded his confession, which I am prepared to show you."

He plugged in a flash drive to an iPad and passed it to Michael. He watched the screen illuminate with the image of a bearded man, dressed in a hospital robe, wearing a knitted skullcap. He was seated at a table, his interrogator sitting opposite him.

"What is your name?"

"I am known as Achmed Bashir."

"Where are you from?"

"Indonesia."

"How did you come to be a prisoner in Israel?"

"I was captured trying to cross the Syrian border into Israel with explosives."

"You were eventually tried as a terrorist, convicted and sentenced to twenty years in prison. Is that correct."

"Yes!"

"What position did you previously have in your native country?"

"I was a laborer working on the construction of a dam in Indonesia."

"While you were working on the dam, did you know a man named Alan Haman?"

"No, not really. I was given his picture and was told that he had to be murdered in the name of Allah. I was paid to kill him and make it look like an accident."

"How did you do this?"

"I moved a large piece of steel so it would fall when he walked under it. When it did I ran to his aid so people would believe I was trying to help him. Nobody knew I had anything to do with his death. I continued to work there as I was told for the next five weeks so no one would be suspicious."

"Who ordered you to kill Alan Haman?"

"A man named Arbry Tamel, and one other whom I knew only as Mhamet Salem, an imam from one of the local mosques."

"Why are you making this confession now?"

"Because I am dying of a brain tumor and have been told that I could receive treatment for it that may save my life. I don't want to die in an Israeli prison. I would rather die in a hospital."

"I've seen enough, I don't want to watch anymore." He was visibly shaken as tears streamed down his cheeks.

"Why don't we take a rest," Ian said.

"No! On second thought, I want to learn more," Michael said while trying to catch his breath.

Amir walked around the table and placed his hands on Michael's shoulders and squeezed them in an act of compassion. Michael reached up and touched his hand before Amir walked back to his seat.

Leon continued. "Arbry Tamel's parents were also murdered in what was made to look like a traffic accident when he was in college, before he was assigned to Indonesia to mentor you. His parents were opposed to his following Islam in the way he was learning it. They believed he was becoming radicalized. Their elimination became necessary because they were American Moslems who were peace-loving people, well respected in their community. His father was a doctor. They did not approve of their son's radicalism. It was believed that they were about to report their son to the authorities. That would have interfered with his indoctrination and their plans. Here's the proof."

He removed two newspaper articles from the Los Angeles *Times*, and the San Francisco *Chronicle* reporting the death of Dr. and Mrs. Habib Tamel. The headlines in the *Times* read "Renowned Doctor and His Wife Killed in Fiery Crash." The story that followed detailed an unexplained traffic accident along the Pacific Coast Highway that left them dead in a flaming crash. He slid them across the table to Michael.

"This is hard to believe," he said with confusion in his voice.

"Believe us, Michael. These people are ruthless," Amir interjected.

"They will stop at nothing to get what they want. They must be stopped and stopped quickly, before they complete their plans," Ian added.

"What happened to Arbry?" Michael asked.

"In due time. First we need to earn your trust and confidence in us. Confidence we hope will lead to your cooperation with us. Michael, we need your help greatly."

"I have a lot to think about. My mind is on overload."

"I can understand. Why don't we stop for today? We can continue tomorrow if you are up to it, Michael?"

"Yes, tomorrow." The pressure in his chest was building. He took in a deep breath and let out a sigh to relieve the tightness he felt from his anxiety.

"Michael, please, I implore of you—we never had these discussions. You are here only on vacation. Please! For your own safety. You have no idea what these people are capable of."

"You have my word, Mr. Ahren, you do. Let me ask you one question: How do you know all these things?"

"Let's just say Israel has the finest intelligence network in the world, as you will soon find out."

Leon Ahren placed everything back into a large expandable folder. He walked over to a wall of bookshelves and pulled them away from the wall. Swinging open like a door, it revealed a large wall safe with two digital combination locks. Ian Sellers entered a six-digit combination in one of the key pads and turned away as Leon Ahren entered his code in the other. Placing the folder inside, Leon closed the steel door and held it closed as a series of steel deadbolts could be heard locking the door.

"If you are up to it, we can have lunch?" Leon asked.

"Maybe in a little while," Michael answered. "I need some air." He took the elevator to the upper deck, and Amir followed behind.

In the elevator, Amir said, "Michael, I am truly sorry. I didn't want it to be like this."

"How long have you known?"

"Not long at all. When I met my father in New York a few months ago, that is when he filled me in on the details."

"I thought your family was from New York all these years?"

"We were. He originally was the deputy ambassador to the United Nations. He returned to Israel seven years ago to take on his current position and head up the investigation. My father still maintains an apartment in the city. He travels back and forth but spends most of his time in Israel. I hardly see him."

"I just pray my father didn't suffer at the hands of these barbaric bastards," Michael said. He felt angry. If Bashir had been in front of him, he would probably have pummeled his face until it was unrecognizable. "I am totally confused. I don't know what to do. How do I tell my mother after all these years?"

"That's entirely up to you," Amir said with compassion in his voice. "Would it do any good at this point to tell her?" Once again he stood behind Michael and placed his hand on his shoulder with a caring touch.

CHAPTER 27

After lunch, which didn't sit very well in Michael's digestive tract, Leon told them that their next port of call was going to be Tel Aviv. "I don't believe you have ever been to Israel, Michael. I am sure you will find it very interesting and educational."

"Do you think with everything you have told me so far that it would be safe for me?"

"Absolutely! You have nothing to fear."

Michael felt apprehensive about visiting Israel. As a young boy he had had it schooled into him that the Jewish people were the enemy: "All Jews are the devil and must be destroyed." He could still hear the words in his mind that had been repeated over and over by his teachers in the madrassa he'd attended. Yet his mother was Jewish; why would his father, a Moslem, marry a Jewish woman? Maybe the visit to Israel would help resolve his inner turmoil. He thought about his mother and could feel the warmth of her touch when he was a little boy and was afraid or awoke from a bad dream. He desperately needed a hug from her.

"I want you to travel around the country to see firsthand what we, as a small nation the size of New Jersey, have accomplished in our short history. Amir will be your guide. I would like you to be my guest at our home for a few days. The accommodations aren't as plush as this yacht, but I'm sure you will find them more than adequate."

Michael reluctantly accepted the invitation. Although he was a little apprehensive at first, he felt reassured that he would be in good hands. His reasoning for his belief was that it was apparent they needed him more than he needed them, so they wouldn't let anything happen to him.

Michael didn't sleep well that night. As he tossed and turned, he kept thinking back to his days as a child in Indonesia. He was playing out in his mind what could have happened to his friend Arbry, and what and how much more Israeli intelligence knew. Then he thought of that fateful day his mother and he learned the awful news of his father's death. All these years he'd believed it was a terrible accident. *Who are these animals? What do they want? More importantly, how far will they go to get it? Why me? There are millions of people in the world. Why is this falling on my shoulders?* He was totally overwhelmed by the flood of emotions that consumed him, from confusion to anguish.

He wanted so desperately to sleep, but his anxiety level wouldn't let him. He kept turning his pillow to the cool side, trying to relax. He was torn between wanting to sleep and wanting the morning to come soon so he could learn more. When it finally did, he was exhausted both physically from lack of sleep and emotionally from all that he had absorbed the day before.

At breakfast Michael hardly ate. He managed to finish half of a cup of coffee and a toasted bagel, but he had trouble getting even that down and didn't know how long he could keep the bagel from coming back up. He hoped the feeling would disappear very soon.

"How are you feeling this morning?" Ian asked of Michael.

"How should I be feeling? You people have managed in one afternoon to turn my entire life upside-down."

"I understand your frustration and anger, but I'm certain your feelings will change shortly."

When they disembarked in Tel Aviv they were met by a caravan of three black Cadillac Escalade SUVs, which would escort them to the minister's residence, forty-three miles away, in a town called Rehavia, an upscale Jerusalem neighborhood not far from the center of the city.

Ian Sellers remained on board the yacht, explaining that he had much work to do and would see them in a few days.

The two-story stone structure, whose color blended in with the surrounding landscape, was surrounded by a twelve-foot-high, ivy-covered concrete wall. A white, pre-formed steel and glass guardhouse, which resembled a large telephone booth with a sliding window, was in place outside the wrought iron gate that protected the entrance. Two armed soldiers in green camouflage uniforms, wearing berets, stood guard at the gate. They were carrying automatic rifles. As they opened the gate to let the vehicles proceed, the soldiers saluted the occupants.

Once inside, Amir gave Michael a quick tour of the home and directed him to his room, which was across the hall from his, a bedroom that he hadn't slept in for years. Michael's room was cheerful. The room had light blue-painted plaster walls. The floor was wood, covered with a Turkish carpet that left a three-foot-wide border around it. A queen-size brass-framed bed was centered on the wall. It was abutted by two wood night stands, which contained brass lamps. On one of the stands there was a clock radio. A single globe fixture was centered in the room; it hung below a ceiling fan that was mounted on the white ceiling. A thirty-six-inch flat screen television was mounted on the wall opposite the bed. Below it was a triple dresser made of oak with brass hardware.

Their first four days were all sightseeing. Leon Ahren wanted Michael to be comfortable and gain a feeling of acceptance in a land that he knew would feel strange to him. Amir, along with a driver and covertly armed escort, was Michael's tour guide. They visited Tel Aviv, Masada, Bethlehem, Yad Vashem, and Jerusalem.

The images at Yad Vashem left him with feelings of anguish. "I only read about the Holocaust in history books. I never could feel the intensity of it until today, when I saw the photos and remnants of this terrifying crime. It really did happen, didn't it, Amir?"

"Yes! Not only were six million Jews murdered, but almost five million other people, including homosexuals, Gypsies, Jehovah's Witnesses, and the disabled. We mourn them all."

Michael thought to himself, *No one could fake those images.* "How could anyone hate people so vehemently just for their religious beliefs, and because they were different?" Michael asked.

"That is why we are such a strong people today. It all comes from Masada. Never again!"

They visited the shops in the old walled city of Jerusalem. Michael noticed that Arabs and Jews worked side by side. He was puzzled by what he saw. "Why are Jews and Moslems working together? I thought they hate each other."

"We don't hate the Moslems, and most Moslems don't hate the Jews. It's only the radical Islamics who want to see us dead. They have hijacked Islam and have turned a beautiful religion into a movement of vile hatred toward us and anyone who will not acquiesce to their beliefs. We love and respect all people as long as they want to live in peace."

His confusion was intensifying. What he was experiencing was entirely contrary to what he had been taught in the madrassa in Indonesia. He felt out of control, as if he were driving a fast-moving car on a patch of black ice. He now saw it for himself and questioned Amir why his early teachers could be so wrong. "Why do they call Jews the devil?" he asked.

"Michael, that's a question we've been trying to answer for hundreds of years. You have no idea how much Israel has contributed to the world," Amir stated.

"If it weren't for Israel, most of the medical devices such as the MRI and CT scans would not be in use today; they were invented here. The pill cam, the first ingestible diagnostic camera, was developed by us. The first cell phone technology was invented in Israel. The Windows NT and XP operating systems were developed here. Israel has the highest number of university graduates per capita in the world. We are a smart and industrious people. I can only summarize it in one word; jealousy!" he said emphatically.

"Look what we have done. We have taken thousands of square miles of barren desert land and turned it into a thriving, industrious paradise. We are a peace-loving people that Radical Islam wants to destroy. Why?"

"I am sorry. I never knew," Michael said.

CHAPTER 28

On the fifth day, Amir and Michael spent a day at the finance minister's office. "I would like to show you how we manage the economy and have you see some of the programs we have put in place. I believe you will find it very interesting," Leon said.

After touring the offices, which were located in the same building as the Knesset, Israel's parliament, the finance minister escorted them into the nerve center of his offices. It was a 7,500-square foot windowless room, which housed hundreds of network computers. The office contained about seventy desks with work stations. Almost all the desks were occupied.

"This is our operations center. From here we can track any sum of money or securities transactions around the world to make sure no one is overloading the monetary system. It is quite a system. We analyze any large movement of funds, especially from subversive groups of former terrorists. Reports are printed and analyzed daily. We have some of the most brilliant economic minds in the world working for us, using some of the most sophisticated computer programs there are. We can track a single $10 payment to your credit card account or a multi-billion-dollar sovereign nation's transfer of funds, and anything in between.

Most of these people have business degrees, many with MBAs, and most of them have worked as analysts with Mossad, the Institute for Intelligence and Special Operations, the equivalent of the U.S. Central Intelligence Agency."

He explained how they monitored large movements of cash in the amount of twenty million dollars or more. "We are secretly tied into every major banking system and securities company in the world. Since the Internet, it has become extremely easy for us to monitor each system."

He picked up a bound folder of reports. "Everything is charted on spreadsheets like these. Amounts that don't conform to our guidelines are investigated as to their legitimacy. For example, this transaction," he pointed to a $200 million transfer from the Royal Bank of Scotland to a division of Prudential Securities in New Jersey, "came from legitimate funds that were converted from commodities and real estate transactions. We just track them and look for unusual activity. Since this transaction doesn't seem out of the ordinary, no further action is needed. Here's another one we looked at: $800 million into a Morgan Stanley account. Those funds came from mining and mineral holdings in Africa, Asia, and the Middle East." Pointing to another transaction, Leon clarified a similar transaction of over $400 million deposited with Merrill Lynch in London. "All aboveboard, totally innocuous. Most of these transactions occurred over ten years ago."

"How many transactions like these do you come across each week?" Michael asked.

"Sometimes two to four a week. With the economy of the world as good as it is, there are a lot of very wealthy people who move money around constantly. Since it doesn't show up in the same place, we don't express concern about it. It's just banking as usual; so we believe."

"This is all very interesting," Michael said. "I would like to learn more about these transactions. There seems to be a lot of money moving around the world. Would it be possible for me to look at some of these reports?"

"Why would you need them?"

"I don't need them, but I'm curious about the movement of money and how it could affect the balance sheets of the banks and brokerage houses that receive the funds."

"I don't see why not. I'll have to redact the individual investors' identities."

"Thank you, Mr. Ahren."

"No problem. I'll bring them home this evening. You two go and do whatever it is you do. I'll see you at dinner."

Amir and Michael left for some more sightseeing.

That evening after dinner, Leon Ahren said to Michael and Amir, "Come into my den. I have the reports you were interested in." Handing Michael a file folder that contained about thirty pages of an Excel file, he said, "These are some of the transactions you wanted to look at. They go back as far as fifteen years. I'm sure you'll find them quite boring."

"Thank you. I'll use them as my bedtime reading. The book I've been reading is also quite boring, so anything would be a change for the better." All three men chuckled.

Michael sat up in bed and read through the reports. He kept going back to three transactions that seemed to jump off the pages at him. All the transfers were from European banks, and all were over $200 million, to three different securities companies—two in the U.S. for a total of one billion dollars, and one in London for 440 million British pounds.

He circled each transaction in pencil and turned in for the night. The next morning at breakfast he said to Leon, "I found those reports to be very interesting. Would it be possible to see some of the older reports for the past ten or more years? I only want to see the ones that contain transactions of more than fifty million dollars, if it's possible to sort them that way. I would like to make up a chart to see how those funds were being distributed after they were transferred."

"What would that show?"

"I'm not sure. It's just something I was thinking about as I read through them last night."

"I don't see why not. I'm sure we can sort them that way. I'll have my secretary print them out for you."

"Thank you.

The next day Leon gave Michael about twelve years of reports, which seemed no different than the ones he had previously reviewed. They contained ninety-two transactions that totaled over $500 billion. Most of the transfers were from European, Chinese, and Saudi holdings that had been deposited with U.S. and European security firms. Michael started to wonder why all this sudden wealth was being spread out among various brokerage firms in different cities in America and Europe. Some of these brokers were with individual branches of larger companies. In some cases, the money was deposited with small, independent brokers. It all didn't make sense to him.

Speaking of his findings with Amir, Michael said, "I wonder where all these funds went. More importantly where they came from. What securities and stocks were being purchased with these funds?"

"That is a great question."

"I wonder if your dad could trace the final destination of these funds, because something doesn't seem right."

CHAPTER 29

L eon Ahren was able to retrieve the information Michael had requested. As he read the reports, Michael discovered that the large cash deposits on the previous report had all gone to purchase large blocks of the common stock of General Electric, General Motors, AT&T, and American and Delta Airlines. Each purchase was for about one-half of one percent of the outstanding shares of each corporation. It was not enough to attract great attention but enough to exercise a large voting block at annual meetings. There were other investments in the major railroads and freight carriers in the U.S.: Union Pacific, Burlington, and Amtrak.

The total of the purchases equated to total control of almost twenty percent of each of the Fortune 500 companies. It seemed a bit odd that the investors from so many different countries of the world would be carrying the same shares in their portfolios. Many of these purchases had been made as far back as thirty years ago.

As Michael reviewed the other transactions from the list, he found they were similar in nature. He concluded that if added together they could totally control the interest of all the corporations in question. And, this was only the beginning. There were other purchases in other Fortune 500 companies that were equivalent to the first. Texaco, Exxon Mobil, Verizon, Rockwell—these were all U.S. corporations. As he looked further, Michael found major investments in Google, Amazon, Kraft Foods, Microsoft, and Apple. In Europe there were investments that, if combined, would control such companies as Philips Electronics, Nestles, Rolls Royce, Volvo, BMW, and Volkswagen. The banking community and investment brokerages were not immune either. It appeared to Michael that these investments were not random but a series of systematic investment plans to control some of the largest companies in the world, industry by industry. All that had to be done was for someone with total control of all these accounts to consolidate the holdings, and no industry would be safe from a takeover.

The total holdings in each company would be equal to about forty percent of each corporation. Warren Buffet couldn't have dreamed of these takeovers. As a matter of fact, some of Berkshire Hathaway's holdings were being targeted.

The next questions in his mind were who and why? Michael needed to speak with Leon Ahren and his superiors. He suspected someone or some group was trying to control everything, one industry at a time.

Michael called Amir's father in his office, "Mr. Ahren, I was reading over the reports you gave me and found something very interesting that I would like to discuss with you. I really believe it is important that I discuss my findings with you."

"I hear an urgency in your voice. Is it something I might be interested in or a theory you have of your own?"

"I can't exactly put my finger on it, but it has given me much food for thought. Something about the investments and the large movements of cash concerns me. It appears to me someone or some group of investors may be trying to take control of some of the largest industries in the world. I really think we should talk."

Michael explained how large investments were being made in major corporations that, if consolidated, could give control of those companies to one individual or a group, who could control it all. "What if all this money was covertly coming from one source and consisted of a large conspiracy to take over the major companies of the world?" he asked.

"It sounds a little farfetched. However, how about if I set up a meeting with some of my co-workers for the day after tomorrow, sometime in the early morning. You could explain your concerns to us all."

"Sure I'm willing to do that," Michael answered.

CHAPTER 30

Two days later, Michael, Amir, and Leon Ahren left together for what Michael thought was going to be a twenty-minute drive to Mr. Ahren's office. However, the drive was longer and not the route they had taken previously. When they approached a guarded gated entrance to a large military-like complex, Leon Ahren identified himself to the guard, who scanned his identity card in his computer. A few seconds later, the large steel gate that was protecting the entrance opened. It allowed them to pull ahead to another gate, which did not open until after the undercarriage of their vehicle was searched with a surveillance mirror and the first gate closed.

"Where are we going?" Michael asked. "This is not your office."

"This is headquarters for Mossad and the Minister of Defense," Leon answered.

"Why are we here? I thought we were going to your office, Michael queried.

"This is where I report to. It seemed fitting that we meet with everyone. You may have discovered something that may be of interest to all of us who have been working on this project. I think you will find our day quite interesting and enlightening."

After passing through a security checkpoint, where Michael and Amir were each given a laminated, clip-on security badge that contained their photos, the three men were escorted to a large conference room. The room was furnished with a twenty-foot-long wood table surrounded by twenty upholstered armchairs. Each end of the room contained a projection screen that was six feet high and ten feet wide. There were two suspended projectors facing each of the screens, which were dwarfed by the twelve-foot-high ceiling. In front of each chair was a leather desk pad, pencils, and a white ruled legal pad. Four pitchers of water and a supply of drinking glasses were neatly placed along the length of the table on silver trays. Two speaker conference telephones were located evenly on the table so they could be heard from anywhere in the room.

Michael felt a little overwhelmed by the size of the room and its contents, especially when the door to enter the room was a foot thick and matched the width of the walls that housed it. This assured that the room was soundproof.

The three men took their seats at the far side of the table, opposite the door. There were large place cards with their names printed on them, indicating where they should be seated. Michael did not recognize the names of the other people who were going to attend the meeting. All he could believe was that this was going to be more than the meeting he was expecting. On the table in front of him he placed a manila folder that contained some of the reports he'd read and his own notes.

Within a few minutes, one by one, the participants entered the room and took their assigned places at the table. Each acknowledged Leon Ahren with a verbal "Shalom," some accompanied with a handshake. The entire group was composed of eleven men, including Michael, Amir, and Leon, and three women.

When the meeting began, Leon Ahren was the first to speak. "Let me tell you why I called this meeting today. With me are my son Amir, whom most of you know, and our house guest, Michael Haman. Michael and Amir attended undergraduate and post-graduate school together. They have been friends for some time. In the short time I have known Michael, I have found him to be a highly intelligent person with a curious mind and a kind heart." Michael felt a little embarrassed at these comments and tried to hide his embarrassment, but his blushing cheeks and broad smile gave it away. It was like the first time he had asked a girl to dance at a high school social.

Leon Ahren continued, "One of the reasons I called you all here today is for you to meet Michael and have him demonstrate his intelligence by presenting to you what he has discovered on his own. Michael the floor is all yours."

Michael rose from his seat to address the group. Opening the folder, he began to express his thoughts and concerns. He was standing in front of some of the most powerful men in the Intelligence Division of the Israeli government. He was overwhelmed and edgy. However, he regained his confidence and tried not to show his nervousness as he started to speak. A green LED light was lit on the conference telephones on the table; at first he didn't notice them.

"I want to thank you for allowing me to express my theory to you, and I want to thank Minister Ahren for calling this meeting. What I have discovered is that the large sums that have been deposited in various investment firms around the world are being invested in the same companies. Each investment is just small enough to fly under the radar of the U.S. Security and Exchange Commission and the regulatory agencies in the European Union and elsewhere. These investments, although not excessive on their own, could be very troublesome and damaging if they turned out to be part of a larger conspiracy to take over large segments of industries by consolidating their holdings.

"Let me see if I can explain it better. Everyone here knows of the largest two amusement parks in the U.S., Disneyland in Anaheim, California and Disneyworld in Orlando, Florida. Walt Disney, the founder and creator, built Disneyland in Anaheim first. What he didn't do was buy up the properties surrounding his theme park. Soon after he opened, low budget motels and souvenir shops opened all around the area and seemed to have denigrated the neighborhood.

So when he decided to build a second park in Orlando, he never revealed his plan. What he did was create numerous corporations that purchased the land around the area. The small purchases flew under the radar. No one was wise to him until he decided to announce his plans for the new park. He wanted to control it all. By consolidating the corporations, he amassed hundreds of thousands of acres of land. More than he needed. He gained control of an entire county in Florida." His throat was dry from being tense. He paused to take a drink of water and continued.

"Now, you may be asking yourself, what that has to do with the investments I have looked at? What if that is happening here? What if someone or some group is doing what Disney did—secretly buying up shares in corporations, only to consolidate them some time in the future and take over entire industries? They could control anything they wanted to. They could control all the energy, shipping, telecommunications, manufacturing, banking, and any other sector they get their hands on. The results could be disastrous. They could shut down food supplies and electricity anywhere they wanted to. They could hold entire populations hostage.

"I'm not saying that is what is happening here, but in your words it doesn't seem kosher. To date I have discovered that almost one trillion dollars has entered the market, and more may be coming. The larger question is, where did all this money originate from?"

"Very interesting," the minister of defense said.

"Mr. Haman, is this all just conjecture on your part, or do you believe it is really possible that this is the intent of these investors?" the intelligence minister asked.

"Yes! I believe it is happening, and please call me Michael. I believe that someone, some group, or maybe even some government is trying to buy up and control the world's economy—for what reason I cannot comprehend."

Suddenly a voice came over the conference telephone. "Michael, this is the prime minister of Israel, Adam Cohen. I have been listening to your presentation." Michael was shocked that the prime minister was listening in.

"I want to congratulate you on your brilliance, young man. You have done in less than a week what has taken us years to discover. I am sorry I am not there to meet you personally, but I am engaged in a matter of state. Perhaps we will meet soon."

"Thank you, Mr. Prime Minister. I am humbled by your compliment." Nervously he said, "I must ask, are you telling me that you have already known this was happening?"

"And more, Michael. You may be surprised at how much we already know. I know you are going to be with us for a few more days. I hope you will be willing to work with us during that time. I am certain we both have much to learn from each other. Finance Minister Ahren will fill you in and brief you on all we know when this meeting is concluded. Until then I hope you would consider our offer to work with us. It could be beneficial to both of us."

"Thank you, Mr. Prime Minister. I will think about it."

"I hope you will consider it wisely. We are always looking for brilliant young minds. Currently I must attend to other duties, so I must say good-bye. I hope you have a pleasant and enlightening day, Michael."

"Thank you, Mr. Prime Minister."

The line went dead.

Michael turned to Amir and asked, "Was that really the Prime Minister?"

Amir nodded *yes*.

Michael looked around the table at the faces of those present. "You all knew of this even before I arrived in Israel?" he asked rhetorically.

"We did, Michael," Minister Ahren answered, although the question needed no answer.

"We wanted a fresh look at our findings from someone on the outside to confirm what we believed. We also believe we can stop it from happening and would like your help. You have an expertise in a subject you may understand better than us."

"What subject is that?"

"I will explain it to you after this meeting. So with that said, I believe we should adjourn."

As the members of the group got up to leave, they congratulated him on his presentation. Some shook his hand while others patted him on the back. Michael felt a little embarrassed as he turned to Amir. His emotions were running wild. It was as though he were on a galloping horse that he had no control of. "You knew this all along? I feel like you used me."

Leon Ahren interjected. "Please don't blame Amir. He was only doing what I asked of him. He is a loving and loyal son. Someday I hope you will have children that you can be proud of as much as I am of him. Please, Michael, keep an open mind for the time being, and wait until I fill you in on what you need to know. You can judge us then. But for now, it's late, and we haven't had lunch."

They proceeded to a cafeteria on the lower level of the building. Leon Ahren excused himself to use the restroom.

"Please, Michael, despite what you believe right now I really am your friend. You are not being asked to help Israel. You are being asked to help save the world from an untenable threat, and Israel is only the vehicle to get you there to help defeat a group that wants to rule the world. It's not just about the Jewish people; it's about all the civilized people in the free world. Please have the open mind you have always had. Keep it open a little while longer, and I promise you will understand soon."

"I hope so," Michael answered with confusion in his voice.

Just then Mr. Ahren reappeared and said, "Let's eat. After lunch you two can be on your way. We'll meet again tomorrow and continue with our discussions. There is much for you to learn. There's not enough time left today to continue. I believe tomorrow you may understand why you were chosen, Michael."

Michael sat bewildered, not knowing what to expect.

CHAPTER 31

The next morning, as they ate breakfast, Leon Ahren turned to Michael and said, "I know this is difficult for you, but the gravity of this situation really gives us no choice. There is much more you need to know. Hopefully by the end of today you will realize how urgent it is for us to proceed with destroying their mission. These people are ruthless. Let's go to the office. I need to show you more."

As the three of them rode in the back of the stretch limousine, Michael sat in the jump seat, facing Amir and his father. He noticed they were not alone. There was a black Mercedes SUV with two men in suits following behind.

Noticing Michael's glances through the rear window, Leon said, "Don't worry. They're with us,"

"Security?" Michael asked rhetorically.

"Yes!"

"Yours or mine?"

"Ours!" was Leon's emphatic answer.

As they entered the conference room, Michael discovered Ian Sellers waiting for them.

"Good morning, Michael."

"Good morning. I didn't know you were joining us."

"I only found out last minute. How have you been faring the past few days?"

"Honestly, it has been a whirlwind. There is so much I now know and so much I don't know and so much I wish I didn't know."

"Hopefully that will all clear itself up for you very soon."

"Why don't we get started," Leon Ahren suggested.

Ian started the conversation. "Michael, the Samson and Delilah Society is not what you were led to believe it is. It was not started as an endowment by an industrialist. There is no Jonathan Wilder. It's a cover story that was devised to hide the true mission of the society.

It has long been suggested that the Skull and Bones at Yale is a branch of the Illuminati, and the society actually controls the U.S. Central Intelligence Agency. It has also been theorized that the Skull and Bones plays a role in a global corporate conspiracy for world domination. That has been found to be pure conjecture, and there is no actual basis for its validity.

"Unlike the Skull and Bones Society, which is controlled by its members, the Samson and Delilah Society is controlled by a faux Islamic group. The Islamic group that started it believe its secret members are part of their conspiracy. They control its structure and are grooming the members to become the CEOs of some of the largest companies in the world, so they believe. They start by finding the best academic students, who are liberal thinkers and easy to persuade, who are destined to become business majors. They then offer them an academic scholarship that is hard to refuse. They have you believe your school expenses are being paid by sponsors, when in reality there are no sponsors; they make them up and funnel the money to you.

"If you succeed academically and they believe you are a true Moslem, one day you are told about a secret society that is inviting you to become a member because of your high academic achievement."

Michael was starting to feel anxious. He could only think of the way he had been recruited for Samson and Delilah, and he knew he fit the mold. He continued to listen to every word, wondering what was coming next, yet somehow he didn't want to know.

Amir continued, "Once you have become a member of the Samson and Delilah Society, then they start working on you by offering you things that are difficult to turn down. When you leave school they secretly get you your dream job. They make sure you move up the corporate ladder until you reach the top. That is when they expect payback.

Michael, the society will literally own you. Then one day they call in the favor. It's at that point that you find you have no choice. Your family will be threatened, and they will ruin you economically. If you don't cooperate, you will find yourself in great danger. That is what they have mandated the society to do. In reality, it is not what we do."

Ian continued from there. "They believe they are like the Illuminati, which is an alleged conspiracy to control world affairs, by masterminding events and planting agents in governments and corporations, in order to gain political power and influence to establish a New World Order. They will stop at nothing until they get what they want. And, what they want is world domination. They make the Illuminati look like child's play."

Leon Ahren interjected, "Michael, they have already begun. You have no idea how many CEOs of Fortune 500 companies they believe are controlled by them. However, it's a false belief, as you are about to discover."

Michael felt a heaviness on his chest. It was as though he were deep under water, kicking for the surface. Every kick of his legs and pull of his arms made him feel like his lungs were about to explode. His anxiety left him out of breath, although he didn't even realize it. He found it hard to speak but managed to get the words out: "Are you telling me I have been living a lie, and my life is being controlled by outside forces?"

"That's exactly what we have been saying," Leon responded. "Only, you haven't been living a lie. You are a brilliant example of what they need—a person who is highly intellectual and eager to succeed in the corporate world. That's what they look for. However, they want only

Islamic believers to further their cause. They have groomed many people in America, Europe, and the rest of the world to do this. They have been surreptitiously using you since you were a boy in Indonesia."

"But I haven't practiced Islam for years," Michael retorted.

Ian interjected; "They don't know that. They believe you still practice the faith because we have convinced them you do," Ian answered.

"Convinced who?"

"What you were not aware of is that within the society there is an inner circle. These are the people who set the policy for the society and make sure the leaders' mandates are carried out."

"What about you, Amir? How do you fit in?"

"They think as a member of the society I am one of them. They believe they control me, but they don't."

Leon Ahren said, "I think I can better explain it this way. Amir is not only my son, he is an agent of the Mossad. He has managed to infiltrate their organization and is a trusted confidant. They believe he is a United States citizen of Moslem descent who is dedicated to their cause. They are totally unaware he is an Israeli."

Ian spoke again. "Michael, I am about to reveal to you a secret that only a select group of people know. You know the Qur'an inside and out, is that not correct?"

"Yes, I do."

"Then you know that Moslems are permitted to lie when it is in their interest to do so, and Allah will not hold them accountable for lying when it is beneficial to the cause of Islam. They can lie without any guilt or fear of accountability or retribution. A lie in the defense of Islam or the furtherance of Islamic principles is approved and even applauded in the Qur'an. It allows for a Moslem to pretend to be someone he is not to deceive his enemy into submission to convert them to Islam. They are the doctrines of religious deception known in the *Qur'an as Taqiyya* and *Kitman*. Do I have that correct?"

"Yes, that's true."

"Michael, the members of the Samson and Delilah Society, with the exception of those in political power who are using the society for their cause, are not who you believe they are. They are not Moslem, as you were led to believe. Besides Amir, all the members are Jewish, pretending to be followers of Islam. They have been carrying out a conspiracy in the name of Islam, pretending to do their bidding to establish world domination. They are getting ready to announce their plan to the world, believing that they control every industry on the face of the earth. One of the most powerful leaders in the world is their leader. He has spent the last forty years putting this plan together."

"Are you telling me that you lied and deceived me just to get me to help you? Why am I so important to you?"

"Because their leader knows who you are and wants you to work with him to help further his plans. He is convinced, because we convinced him when they tried to radicalize you as a young man, that you are a true believer in their cause. He may not reveal himself to you with his true identity, but I want you to know who he is," the finance minister said.

He reached across the table and picked up a TV remote control. As he pressed a button on the control, the screen on the wall lit up with a picture of Arbry Talem. It was the same photo Michael had been shown on the yacht. "You know who that is? – It's Arbry Talem."

"Yes!"

"Do you know who this man is?" Another photo appeared.

"Of course! That's the vice president of the U.S., Barry Melat."

"Yes it is. It is also Arbry Talem. They are one and the same," Leon said emphatically.

"How can that be?"

The next image showed both photos side by side. "Arbry Talem, without the beard and with a little plastic surgery to augment his nose and eyes, is Barry Melat. His name is an anagram. He had his makeover right after he left Indonesia before returning to the states."

Michael sat there in shock. "I can't believe what I'm seeing. Are you certain?"

"We have his DNA. There is no mistake."

"There is a lot we know about him. For one thing, he never married. He didn't want a wife or family interfering with his plans."

Ian interjected, "He is about to propose legislation that will threaten the balance of corporate America and the world in a way that has never been imagined. It will destroy competition in America, Europe, and the Far East, all in the name of Allah. It is the Illuminati on steroids."

Leon Ahren continued, "Michael, what we have been telling you is nothing new. We have been working surreptitiously for years to get inside their organization and defeat them from within. It has not been an easy task. We have people in place who work for us but are helping them plan their next move surreptitiously. We are doing this to build their trust and confidence, to make them believe their plan is becoming operational. There are things we have done that we are not proud of, but they had to be done to move things along so we can defeat them."

"What sort of things are you speaking about?"

"Michael, I believe I can trust that what I am about to tell you will not go beyond this room."

"You have my word. You can trust me," he said emphatically.

"Do you remember when Vice President Karlin died? His autopsy showed it was from natural causes. It was not! He was assassinated. It had to be assured that the progression of political events that followed would lead to what the administration is today.

"A member of the staff of Vice President Melat is one of our agents. He is a holdover from two previous vice presidents, who has been there for over a decade. He is the only other person in the U.S., except for Barry Melat and a secretive handful of others, who knows what really happened to Joseph Karlin; and, now you know.

"It was concluded after many difficult deliberations that his elimination had to be carried out. Believe me, no one is proud of what had to be done. We knew that they only way for the progression of political appointees to occur that would put Barry Melat in place was to eliminate Karlin. Joseph Karlin was an extraordinary man, who unfortunately had to become collateral damage. Our man in Washington has never gotten over his death."

Ian took over the conversation from there. "Michael, in about four weeks you are going to become my right hand man and confidant. Sometime after that, there will be a meeting with Steven Moslek, John Malcom, Amir, you, and myself. For the first time since you knew him in Indonesia you will come face to face with Arbry Talem. As Barry Melat, vice president, he is looking to add another person to his staff from the Society, who can help him carry out their plan. We will make sure that you are that person. At this meeting you must charm him and convince him that no one is better for that task than you. Don't be too convincing—just whet his appetite a little. I know you can handle it. I have faith in you. If we didn't believe you could do it, you would not be here with us today."

"How can I help? Where do we begin?"

"We have already begun," said Leon. "If you are serious about joining us, your training will begin the day after tomorrow."

Michael felt overwhelmed and frightened. Two weeks ago he had just been a young man on vacation. Now suddenly he found himself becoming part of a team that needed to destroy an organization before it destroyed the world. He knew what he had to do. He was about to jump into an arena as one of the players in a game of international espionage.

"What am I supposed to do? What do you expect of me? What if I am discovered?" He had so many questions.

"You have nothing to do except whatever Vice President Melat wants you to do. You just carry out his orders and complete the task to the best of your ability. You will report to us everything he asks of you. We will handle the rest. We just need to know what he is planning before it is carried out."

"How do I do that? Do you give me a secret decoder ring to wear?" he asked with a nervous laugh.

The three men laughed with him. "Not a bad idea, but we don't have a ring for you. Your contact will be our man inside the vice president's office. He is a Secret Service officer named Ron Moss, whom the vice president trusts emphatically. He believes Moss is a collaborator. Moss knows as much about you as we do. Not only will he be your contact, he is also there to protect you, which we don't see a need for. Do you have any questions?"

"No! But you do realize how frightened and upset I am? My stomach is feeling so upset I am ready to vomit."

"It's understandable," Leon said. "You are being placed in a precarious position. Unfortunately for you, it was your surreptitious handling by the enemy that brought you to our attention and led you here. I don't envy you in the least. But fortunately for us you are here. I…I mean we," he corrected his words, "know that you will be okay. Their plan must be defeated and brought to an end before it is completed, so they never gain world dominance."

Leon also knew that the hateful feelings Michael now had for the vice president, since being told of his father's murder, would help to reduce his agitated feelings and help him carry through his mission.

"Why don't you just announce to the world what their plans are? If you have the evidence as you say you do, isn't that enough to put this madness to an end?"

"Unfortunately it's not that simple. We are Israel. The world has never believed us in the past, even though we have been accurate time after time. Why would they start believing us now? We must prove it to them, let them see it for themselves, and put it to an end. Then they will believe it," the finance minister said.

"Michael, in two days you will board the yacht to continue your vacation. However, it will be cut short so you can arrive back in the U.S. to begin your new job. I probably will not be in contact with you personally until we have completed our mission. If you need to reach me for anything, you can do it through Amir or Ian. Good luck, Michael."

"Thank you Minister Ahren. I think I will need it."

"I am sure you will do fine." As the men started to disperse from the conference room, Leon Ahren turned to Amir and said, "For now you need to relax and clear your head. Amir, why don't you and Michael take time at the beach? After all, you are on vacation."

There was another meeting going on that day. The board of directors of the General Electric Corporation decided to tender an offer to Philips Electronics. Three days later, Philips would accept their offer. The two companies' combined would become the largest distributor of appliances and electronics in the world. Eleven months later, General Electric would become the parent company of Boeing, Rockwell, and Northrop. They would become the largest publicly traded corporation on the New York Stock Exchange.

CHAPTER 32

A week after arriving back in New York, Michael took his position with Ian Sellers as vice president of executive administration; a new position created for him. Amir was hired by Steven Moslek as vice president of acquisitions.

One month later, in early-September, Ian arranged a private meeting in Washington, DC to meet with them and a political leader. The men were apprehensive about the meeting, especially Michael. He was nervous and somewhat anxiety ridden, but he knew what he had to do.

At the Hay Adams Hotel, where they were staying, it was arranged that they would have a private dinner. They assembled in the Lafayette dining room. The table in the separate windowless private room was set for six. As they entered the room, two Secret Service agents greeted them at the door. They were asked to raise their arms parallel to the floor as, one by one, they were scanned with a portable metal detector. To no one's surprise, nobody beeped. As the agents left the room to take their places on the other side of the door, Amir turned to Steven Moslek and asked, "Who is coming for dinner?" Before Steven could answer, Michael mumbled, "I believe I know and wish I didn't know."

The four of them took their places at the table to await the other guests. Amir repeated, "Who are we expecting?

"Just an important member of the society you haven't met yet. I know you will recognize him. John Malcom will be with him," Steven answered with some vagueness, as if to keep the suspense growing.

"However, I must caution you that you will probably hear things tonight that must remain completely confidential. You are about to learn how powerful the society can be. Our guest is a product of the society, which has elevated him to the stature he enjoys today."

About three minutes later, the double doors to the dining room were opened by the same two agents who had scanned Michael and Amir earlier. Entering the room first was a man in a navy blue suit who quickly scanned the room with his eyes. He glanced at Michael for what seemed like an eternity, then turned to the two agents at the door and nodded his head to signify that everything was all right. At that moment in walked Barry Melat, vice president of the U.S., followed by John Malcom. The four dinner guests immediately rose to their feet.

The vice president gently placed his hand on the shoulder of the man in the suit and said, "Thank you, Ron. You can wait outside." Secret Service agent Ron Moss left the room to join the other agents on the far side of the door.

Ian greeted the vice president as he and Steven shook his hand. "Mr. Vice President, I would like you to meet Amir Ahren and Michael Haman, two young, brilliant, and trusted society members."

The vice president greeted both boys with a hearty handshake and a pat on the shoulder. He expressed how glad he was to meet them. "John Malcom has told me a lot about both of you. I am glad you agreed to join us this evening. We have much to discuss."

Michael suddenly felt a chill come over him as though he were standing in front of a walk-in freezer and someone had just opened the door. It was a feeling that he didn't like. The man in front of him, whom he hadn't seen in over sixteen years, had once been his mentor, yet was someone who'd had a hand in his father's death. He was filled with rage. Nevertheless he knew he had to keep it within. He felt dirty after shaking the vice president's hand. However, he was on a mission and had to act accordingly.

The vice president looked at Michael and thought, *How long has it been? It must be fourteen or fifteen years. He hasn't changed much.* He felt proud of himself that he had groomed him to be the man he is today.

If he only knew.

They started with their appetizers, and when the waiters left the room, Steven asked John if they had discussed the group's proposal. "Yes, we did, and I think Bar…I mean the Vice President can answer that."

Michael and Amir picked up that this was more than a meet-and-greet casual dinner.

"Well, because of the amount of mergers and acquisitions that have taken place over the last decade, and, with all the cooperation between corporate America and the global community, we want to make it easier for mergers and acquisitions to take place. So I am proposing to the president that we repeal both the Sherman and Clayton Antitrust Acts. With the influence I have with the Congress, I don't believe it would be a problem. I am certain I can get it through the House, and no doubt the Senate, with little or no opposition. I'm sure the president would sign it."

Michael couldn't believe what he was hearing. Is this the legislation Ian was speaking of when they met with Leon Ahren? Repealing those two acts would pave the way for unbelievable monopolies. *Those laws have stood on the books for the longest time. Why do we need to repeal them?* he thought to himself. Then he asked it out loud. "Why!" He was almost shouting in defiance. He was playing his part well. Ian looked on with some pride as he thought to himself, *Good job, Michael.*

"Why what?"

"Why repeal them?"

"Yeah! Why now?" Amir added. He tried to act as troubled as Michael.

"Because without them, our plans can move forward more quickly."

"What plans?"

"The plan to become the most powerful nation on earth by controlling the entire corporate structure. Once we do that, we will never need a military. If need be, we can just starve our enemies into submission."

"But the world has been at peace for the past fifteen years. Military budgets have been cut around the world. Every nation that had nuclear weapons has given them up. Why do we need to take over the world?"

"We don't want to take it over. We just want to be in position in case we need to. It was like the Reagan Doctrine decades ago, 'Peace through Strength,' only this way we can obtain it without firing a single shot. How long do you think the current peace will last—another ten years, twenty? It can't go on forever. We must be prepared. This doesn't mean we will use starvation as a weapon; just the threat of it will keep the peace. Like Reagan's Star Wars initiative. It brought the Soviet Union to its knees without even launching one satellite. We just need to be prepared."

"I'm not sure that's the way to go about keeping the peace," Michael stated, as both he and Amir seemed to be playing their characters very well without raising any suspicion.

The vice president turned to John Malcom and asked, "Have they read the entire plan?"

"Not yet. We were going to get to it very soon."

"Gentlemen, I know you will understand it much more clearly once you read the entire platform. There's plenty of time. What the vice president is proposing couldn't happen for at least a year, and by that time, who knows what will happen. Opposition may grow to the point that repealing the Sherman and Clayton Acts won't be possible. Let's not put the cart before the horse," John said.

"Okay! I will read it with an open mind," Michael responded.

"That's the answer I wanted to hear. Shall we continue with dinner? I'm hungry," the vice president said.

They completed their dinner and were into dessert when the vice president excused himself and left for the evening. The group rose from their chairs once again as Vice President Melat walked around the table and said good night while shaking everyone's hand. When he reached for Michael's hand, Michael got that same chilled feeling he had earlier in the evening. Only this time it didn't pass as quickly.

"I like you, Mr. Haman. I would enjoy meeting you again. I like the way you think. I believe you will accomplish great things."

"Thank you, Mr. Vice President." He wanted to vomit.

"Good night, gentlemen," Melat said as he left the room with Agent Moss ahead of him.

"Well, that was interesting," Michael said. "I hope I didn't embarrass myself."

"Not at all. We like open debate like that. It makes for a healthy relationship among friends. Don't give it a second thought," John said as if to appease him.

A week after the meeting, Michael received a telephone call in his office. The voice on the other end of the line said, "Michael Haman, please hold for Vice President Melat."

"Michael, this is Vice President Melat. I wanted to let you know, young man, that I was extremely impressed with you the other evening at our dinner meeting. Michael, I was wondering if it would be possible for you to come to Washington to meet with me. I have a proposal that I think would be of interest to you."

"I don't see why not! When would you like to meet, sir?"

"How about next Tuesday? I will have a government plane pick you up at LaGuardia Airport at the Marine Air Terminal. They will fly you into Dulles Airport, where my Secret Service agent, Ron Moss, will pick you up and bring you to my office. Let's say 8:30 A.M. at the terminal. We should have you back in New York in time for dinner."

"Thank you, Mr. Vice President. I'm looking forward to meeting with you."

"See you then, Michael. Have a good day."

Michael went into Ian Sellers office and closed the door. He looked up from his desk and asked, "What's up?"

"The fish has taken the bait. Talem, I mean Melat, wants to meet with me next Tuesday in Washington."

"Good! Did he say what he wants you to do?"

"No, just that he had a proposal he wanted to discuss with me."

"He probably wants you to take on the position of his legislative assistant. If that's it, you will be right in the mix where we want you. I'll let Leon know."

"I can't say I'm not a little anxious about it."

"It's to be expected. I know you will be fine."

CHAPTER 33

After a sixty-five-minute flight from New York's LaGuardia Airport to Dulles, the plane was met on the tarmac. Michael walked down the steps of the Grumman G-5 to the handshake of Ron Moss. "Welcome, Mr. Haman. Glad to see you again. I hope you had a good flight?"

"Yes, it was comfortable and quick."

"Good! Let's not keep the vice president waiting too long." As they walked to the black Cadillac SUV parked about thirty yards away, Ron Moss said to Michael in a whisper, "Don't talk about anything in the vehicle but the weather. Our driver is not one of us."

Michael understood and nodded once in agreement.

After clearing security and receiving his visitor's badge, which hung around his neck on a lanyard, they walked through the lobby entrance to the vice president's office. Ron Moss knocked twice on the closed door. "Yes!" A voice could be heard from the other side.

Moss opened the door and said, "I have Mr. Haman for you, Mr. Vice President."

"Thank you Ron. Please show him in."

When Michael was ushered in by Agent Moss, Vice President Melat was seated in a large, high backed black leather chair at his desk. John Malcom was also there; he was seated to the right of the vice president's desk in a gold upholstered armchair. The light blue carpet that covered the floors accented the blue walls. Perpendicular to Melat's desk was a dark blue sofa and mahogany coffee table. In the corner of the room was an American flag, which was mounted on a wooden pole attached to a brass base. Michael was surprised to see John Malcom there. As Michael entered, the two men rose and greeted him.

"I'm glad to see you again, John. I wasn't aware you would be at this meeting."

"The vice president asked me to attend."

"I suspect you had a good trip, Michael," Melat said as he walked around his desk to shake Michael's hand.

Michael consciously used a firm handshake. It was his way of exhibiting strength of character. What he really wanted to do was squeeze the life out of Melat.

"Yes, my flight was good, thank you."

"Would you like anything to drink? Water, coffee, or tea?"

"Water would be fine. Thank you."

The vice president picked up his telephone and said to his secretary, "Could we have some water for our guest please?"

Pointing to the sofa, Melat said, "Michael, please have a seat. I would like to get started. I have a busy schedule today and want to get right to the point and the reason for wanting to meet with you." The vice president spoke as John took a seat flanking Michael from his right. The vice president returned to his desk and recaptured his seat there. "John and I have been friends for years and members of the society together. We have discussed you ardently and are very impressed with your intellect and you as a person."

"Thank you, Mr. Vice President. I am humbled by your sincerity." He played his part extremely well and tried to forget he was talking to the man who was responsible for the death of his father, if only for the sake of his mission, he thought. The vice president's secretary was now presenting Michael with a silver tray containing a crystal glass of water with ice.

"Thank you," he said as he removed the glass from the tray and took a sip. She placed a coaster on the table and left. Michael placed the glass on the coaster and sat back, more relaxed.

"I would like to discuss the possibility of you leaving Ian Sellers and taking a position with me. I am in need of an executive legislative assistant. The job involves mostly research and writing proposed legislation for me. It includes an annual salary of $150,000, a government apartment, an expense account, medical insurance, and a full, vested pension after two years. Of course, your tenure will last only as long as I am in office, which will be for another three years, and eight more after that if all goes as planned. If I am elected president, I will have no problem keeping you on. After that, you can write your own ticket. Is that something that interests you?"

Michael didn't want to seem too quick to answer. He wanted to sink the hook in a little deeper. "That's a lot to think about. I really like what I'm doing. I never thought of myself in a government job."

"Don't think of it as a job. Think of it as serving your country."

John interjected, "Michael, also think of it as paying it forward—something the society expects of you."

"Then I guess I don't have much of a choice, do I? When do I begin?"

"How long would it take you to wrap things up in your present position with Ian?"

"Probably a few weeks."

"Then it's settled. You can start at the beginning of next month, the first Monday of October. That gives you three weeks."

Barry Melat walked around from his desk placed his left hand on Michael's right shoulder and shook his hand once again and congratulated him. He looked Michael up and down like a haberdasher fitting him for a new suit and thought to himself, *He has no idea who I really am. If only he knew.* "I hope you recognize the significance of your decision, young man? You are going to go places here."

"Congratulations, Michael," John said. "This is a big step for you in your career."

The vice president picked up his phone once again and asked his secretary to come in. When she entered the room, he said to her, "Please have Mr. Haman fill out all the necessary forms to start his employment with us."

Turning to Michael, he said, "Unfortunately, John and I have a meeting to attend, so I must leave you. Agent Moss will get you back to the airport whenever you are ready. I will see you in three weeks. Good luck, Michael"

"Thank you, Mr. Vice President. I won't disappoint you."

Then he asked where the restroom was. He desperately wanted to wash the dirt from his hands.

After completing all the necessary forms, Michael was ready to head back to New York. Agent Moss escorted him back to Dulles Airport. The last thing Ron Moss said to Michael as he was boarding the plane was, "Michael, trust me—you are in good hands."

"I'm sure I am."

When Michael arrived back in New York he called Ian.

"How did it go with the Vice President?"

"The fish is on the hook. I'm sorry, but I'm leaving you in three weeks."

"Make it two. You'll need a week off to rest and recharge your batteries."

CHAPTER 34

After spending the weekend moving into his newly furnished apartment, Michael was eager to get started. His first day on the job was uneventful. He spent most of the first morning meeting the people he would be interacting with and finding his way around. He settled into his new office, a twelve by fifteen carpeted room with an L-shaped desk, black leather desk chair, and two leather side chairs. Although he had much trepidation about his job, he believed if he kept busy his fears would subside. He knew he could not overlook his mission.

His duties entailed reviewing proposed legislation, which for the most part concerned taxes, corporate regulation, and trade. He would write reports for the vice president on how he believed the legislation, if enacted, would affect business and the economy.

On his twelfth day on the job, the vice president asked him to attend a meeting with him and President Amanti. The vice president explained to Michael that the topic of the meeting would be his proposal to appeal the Sherman and Clayton Anti-Trust Acts. "If he is receptive to the idea, I would like you to write the legislation. I believe you are up to the task. What do you think?"

"I think I could handle it. I'll have to do some research, but I don't believe it will be a problem."

When they entered the Oval Office, the president was standing by the window looking out beyond the Rose Garden at the changing leaves on the trees surrounding the White House. He turned and walked toward the vice president and Michael. "Barry, good to see you. This must be Michael Haman, your new legislative assistant. I've heard a lot about you, young man. I'm glad you could attend this meeting." He shook Michael's hand.

"Thank you, Mr. President. It's an honor to meet you."

"Michael, I believe we have a mutual friend."

"Who would that be, Mr. President?"

"Ian Sellers of Verizon. We've been friends for many years. When we spoke last week he mentioned that you would be working with the vice president."

"Yes! I'll be glad to say hello for you when I speak with him next."

The three men took their seats on two sofas that were facing each other, perpendicular to the president's desk. Michael and the vice president were on one sofa; the president sat opposite them. Michael intentionally sat as far away from the vice president as he could. He could not eliminate from his mind and heart the knowledge of who this man really was. The farther away from him he was at all times, the better. He was trying to subdue his inner rage.

"I read your proposal on the repeal of the Sherman and Clayton Acts. I find it very interesting. Do you really believe it will lead to better cooperation between corporate America, Europe, Asia, and the rest of the world?"

"Yes I do. Look at what has happened in Europe and here at home over the past several years. There really have not been any runaway monopolistic events that have caused an imbalance in the economy. Actually most companies have been more in tune with consumers' needs with regard to pricing and quality than ever before. Relieving the barriers to corporate mergers would speed up the process and allow more companies to consolidate their holdings quickly."

The president turned to Michael and asked, "What do you believe, young man.?"

"I believe removing some of the barriers of government regulation would let more companies integrate with greater ease with far less litigation, which could lead to more cooperation in the world economically.

Companies over the last decade have finally learned that corporate greed can be expensive. There may be a new corporate culture to prove to the world that they can provide what people want, while at the same time not worrying about the bottom line. Just think about the auto industry over the past few years. When was the last time you heard of a recall? Manufacturers are learning it is cheaper to do it right the first time with better quality control, instead of cutting corners and spending twice as much repairing it. There is no race to get to market before the next guy. It all goes to the bottom line.

Moreover, consumers are learning to have more trust in the products they are buying, thereby having more trust in the companies that manufacture them. It is trust that builds confidence, which is much more prevalent in the world, quite different then it was twenty years ago. Isn't that what everyone wants?"

Then, with a hint of humor in his voice, he added, "Mr. President, it has even spread to the political arena."

Looking toward the vice president, the president said with a big smile, "Smart young man you have here. I think he's a keeper."

"Thank you," Michael interjected. "I had some great teachers along the way."

"Humble too." The president added.

"Then repeal it shall be. Can you get it through the House and Senate?"

"I don't believe that will be a problem," Melat said. "I'm sure we have the votes."

"Then write the legislation."

The meeting adjourned, and both men left the Oval Office. The vice president said, "Michael, let's go to my office. I would like to talk to you." Once inside Melat's office, he closed the door behind him and asked Michael to take a seat on the sofa. He sat to Michael's right in an armchair. "I must say, young man, you were brilliant in there. I don't think I could have sold it to the president without your input. You are truly amazing."

"Thank you, sir."

"No! Thank *you*. I want you to write the legislation. After what I just witnessed in the Oval Office, I know you are up to the task. You will have your work cut out for you. Let's see if we can have this ready in a few weeks. I want you to make it a priority."

"I'll give it my best."

"Do you have any plans for dinner?"

"Not really."

"Good. I want you to come to my house for dinner. I believe my chef is preparing Baked Rosemary Chicken with all kinds of Mediterranean side dishes. It's my favorite meal. He always prepares much too much, so there is always plenty of food. I won't take no for an answer. It will give us some time to talk and get to know each other a little more."

He desperately wanted to decline the invitation, but knew for the sake of his mission he couldn't. He was also curious what Melat wanted to talk about. "Okay, what time?"

"Let's say six-thirty. This way we can say our evening prayers together before dinner."

He hadn't been expecting that last comment. Michael became anxious and hoped he remembered his prayers. *This may be a test*, he thought.

"I'll see you then. I'll take a taxi."

"No need to. I'll have Ron pick you up at six. That will give you plenty of time in case there is any traffic. You know how Washington can be in the evening. And make it casual. Jeans are fine. You know what," he added. "It's three o'clock. Why don't you leave for the day. This way you can relax a little before dinner."

"Thank you, Mr. Vice President. I would like to do that."

Michael went into his office to check his phone messages and email. There was nothing that couldn't wait until tomorrow. Feeling a little apprehensive, he grabbed his jacket and left for the day.

When he arrived at his apartment, he immediately went to his bookcase and removed a copy of the Qur'an. He wanted to brush up on the prayers that he hadn't said in years. He recited them from memory and then checked the Holy Book. "Just like riding a bike," he said aloud.

CHAPTER 35

Ron Moss picked Michael up on time. When he got into the car, Michael immediately smelled the fresh scent of carpet shampoo. Ron apologized before Michael had a chance to comment. "Sorry for the smell; they had it cleaned today, inside and out."

"Are you kidding? You should have been in the taxi I rode in Istanbul," he said while laughing.

After making the obligatory small talk. Moss asked, "What does Melat want to meet with you about?"

"I really don't know. I think he is testing me to see how faithful I am. I doubt he is going to reveal himself to me. It would be political suicide. Besides, things seem to be going the way he wants. Why would he jeopardize his plans?"

"Okay! Just be careful, Michael."

"I'm not really worried. Ron, just to let you know, it looks like we convinced President Amanti to go along with the repeal of the Sherman and Clayton Acts. Melat wants me to write the legislation. So let Ian know."

"No problem."

They arrived at the gate of the Naval Observatory, checked in with the sentry, and proceeded to the vice president's residence.

The white nineteenth century house at Number One Observatory Circle in northwestern Washington, D.C. had been built in 1893. Before that, vice presidents and their families lived in their own homes, but the cost of securing their private residences grew significantly. In 1974, Congress agreed to refurbish the house as a home for the vice president. The first vice president to move in during his term in office was Walter Mondale.

Two Secret Service agents were standing guard out front and escorted Michael to the front door. Melat answered the door himself. He was dressed in blue jeans and a white oxford shirt. His feet were covered in beige socks and brown loafers. "I'm glad you could make it. It will give us a chance to talk a little without the phones ringing or people barging into our offices."

Just then one of the kitchen help entered, carrying a tray with two glasses and a pitcher of iced tea. "Sir, may I offer you some," he said.

"That would be fine," Michael answered.

Melat led Michel across the reception hall to the sitting room. "Sit. Let's talk. We'll pray before dinner."

Michael sat in a single chair by himself. He wanted to stay as far away from the vice president as he could. He had no doubt that Melat knew who he was; he was certain of that. He was just as certain that Melat was not suspicious that Michael knew who Melat really was. He had to choose his words wisely during whatever conversation was about to take place. He had to build up Melat's trust in him.

"Michael, I want to compliment you on your work with me. You have shown me that you are ready to move up and take on more responsibility. The feedback I have received from everyone who has met you has been extremely positive. They are all impressed with your abilities. You have done yourself proud, young man."

"Thank you, Mr. Vice President."

"Michael, I want to discuss a few things with you—some personal things. Before we brought you into the society we did our homework. As you know, we conduct due diligence on every prospective member. Here is what I know about you. Your childhood was spent in Indonesia. Your father was a Moslem and wanted you to learn about his faith. You studied Islam passionately and can recite the Qur'an from memory. Your mother was a Jew. Your father married outside of his faith. It happens sometimes, so be it. According to our faith, he should have tried to convert her, but he didn't. I don't hold that against him. Look what their marriage produced; we have you. You do know that according to the Qur'an the son of a Moslem male is a Moslem no matter what faith his mother is."

He thought to himself, *My mother is not "a Jew." She is Jewish. Don't make it sound dirty. Don't disparage my mother, you murderous bastard. I carry her blood, not his."* As much as he missed his father and still loved him, he had to call it as it was. His anger was growing. He was seething inside. But he knew he had to control his feelings.

"Yes, I know. As you said, I know the Qur'an quite well," Michael said.

"What about your beliefs? Do you believe the Twelfth Imam is destined to return some day?"

Michael took a moment to gather his thoughts. He knew he was being tested. Not wanting to give the vice president anything to be suspicious about, he answered. "Yes, I believe he is destined to return."

"I knew you were a true believer. Come, let us pray."

They stood up, moved to the center of the room, faced east, knelt down, and prayed the covenants of the Qur'an. When they had finished their prayers, Melat said, "Let's eat." They moved into the dining room, where they were served by the staff. They made small talk during dinner, which lasted about fifty minutes. They talked about sports and growing up in Chicago and Atlanta. Michael desperately tried to steer the conversation away from anything political. He tried to keep this meeting light.

"Let me show you the rest of the house," the vice president offered. He led Michael through the reception hall to the stairs that led to the second floor. There was a window on the staircase that contained a clear, etched, leaded glass replica of the vice-presidential seal.

"There are only two bedrooms on the second floor, plus a study and den," Melat explained. When he showed him the master bedroom, Michael suddenly felt a chill come over him. It was like walking into a refrigerated storage room in a big store, where fruits and vegetables were kept chilled. He thought to himself, *This is where it all began.*

After the tour they returned to the sitting room, where they were served tea. Michael refused dessert, claiming he was watching his weight. He really wanted this evening to end quickly and didn't want dessert to drag it on. The less time he spent with Melat, the better. He excused himself shortly thereafter, explaining that he had much to do at home and wanted to get into the office early to get started on the new legislation.

"I understand. I'm glad you're eager to get started. The faster we get it done, the better for all."

All who? This man is ruthless, Michael thought to himself.

Melat called Agent Moss and told him Michael was ready to leave. Moss arrived about seven minutes later to escort him home.

"Good night, Michael. I'll see you tomorrow." Melat said.

"Good night, Mr. Vice President."

Michael got into the waiting car. "So how was it?" Moss asked.

"Fine. But I was right, it was a test. He was testing my loyalty to Islam."

"Do you think you passed?"

"With flying colors."

"Great! I'll let Ian know."

The rest of the ride home was quiet, Michael was trying to absorb the evening to see if he could pick up any other clues that the vice president might have revealed, but couldn't think of any.

When he recalled his conversation with Melat about his mother, he began to cry.

"Are you all right?" Moss asked.

"I'll be okay. It was just something that bastard said about my mother that upset me."

He couldn't wait to get into the shower and remove the stench.

CHAPTER 36

It was 8:05 the next morning when Vice President Melat walked into Michael's office. Michael started to get up from his chair. "Don't get up," Melat said. "You're in early." He noticed the large number of folders and books spread out over Michael's desk and on the floor. "What time did you get here?"

"I got in at about six forty-five. I couldn't sleep last night. I was thinking about our conversation and how quickly I could get all this done."

"What about our conversation?"

"Not too much, just about how much you know about me and how much we seem to think alike."

"I'm glad you feel that way. I believe we can do great things together. If everything goes as planned you can really go places...if you are willing to take the ride with me."

"I don't see why not, but first things first. I want to get this legislation written so you can have it ready before Congress recesses."

"Okay—don't let me hold you up. If you need anything, just let me know." Then, banteringly, he chided, "Get to work."

Michael was obsessive about his work for the next three weeks. He could be found in his office by 7:30 each morning and sometimes didn't leave until 8:00 in the evening. Many days found him working through lunch. He was exhausted. Many nights when he arrive home he just kicked off his shoes and fell asleep with his clothes on. However, he knew he had to get this done so the all the pieces would start to come together.

He was unsure if he was working so hard for his mission or his belief that his father, a peace-loving man, was watching over him. He knew his father's beliefs were not those of Melat and his conspirators. He also knew how proud of him his father would have been when this was over, if he were still alive. Then he thought about his mother and how loving and compassionate a woman she was, and how difficult it had been for her after his father's death. He wanted to…No he needed to talk to her. It had been at least two weeks since they had spoken last. He called her. "Hi, Mom. How are you?"

"I'm fine, Michael. It's good to hear your voice."

"I apologize for not having called you in a while, but I've been involved in a large project. I'm working day and night to get it done, so forgive me. I miss you, and you know how much I love you."

"Yes I do, I know you're doing important work, and I know how time can fly by when you're busy. I didn't want to call and disturb you."

"You could never disturb me. You know that. Mom, I've been thinking a lot about Dad lately. I really miss him and wish he could see what I'm doing. I want to make him proud."

"I'm sure he knows. Your father has always watched over us. I can feel his presence all around me."

"I know, Mom. I feel him, too."

"Hey, guess who is going to be in town in a few weeks?" he asked rhetorically, then answered his own question: "Amir! We haven't seen each other in almost six-months."

"That's terrific. How is he doing?"

"He's doing great. We speak at least every two weeks. He really loves his job."

They made small talk for a few minutes and, when they ran out of things to say, they said good-bye to each other. Michael added that he would call her in a few days.

It took twenty-three days, working six days a week, for Michael to complete his research and prepare the documents that would be needed to draft the legislation. When he finished his work and read it over, he felt like an artist who had just completed a painting and was standing back from the easel to admire his work. He prepared a back-up copy of his work on a blank flash drive and placed it in his pocket.

When he presented the documents to the vice president for his approval, Michael had mixed feelings about what he was preparing for. Repealing the Sherman and Clayton Anti-Trust Acts could have a devastating effect on the economy of the world, not just the United States. On the other hand, not helping to move Melat's plan along could only prolong the conspiracy. He felt torn. He was being pulled in two directions at the same time. He only hoped it was the right thing.

The vice president was ecstatic when Michael presented his work to him. "You finished this in record time. I'm totally shocked. I am sure we can get this edited and moved along quickly."

"I already had it edited, but one more look at it couldn't hurt," Michael said. "If you haven't got anything pressing, I'd like to leave for lunch. My former roommate, Amir, is in town, and we're meeting at Del Frisco's. We haven't seen each other in months."

"The last time I saw him was at a society meeting about six months ago. Send him my regards.

Why don't you take the rest of the day off? You really deserve it. You worked your ass off on this for me. This way you can spend more time with Amir. How long will he be in town?"

"He's leaving tomorrow. He flew in last night. He had some business with some D.C. attorneys."

"Why don't you let my driver drop you off? It will be faster for you. The metro could be a pain this time of day."

"Thank you, Mr. Vice President."

When Michael entered the restaurant, he looked to see if Amir had arrived. As he moved down the row between the tables and booths he saw him sitting in a booth next to a window that overlooked the street. Noticing Michael walking toward him, Amir got up and met him halfway. They hugged and heartily patted each other on the back. Michael kissed him on the cheek.

"I can't believe we're here. How long has it been?" Michael asked.

"Almost a year."

"It seems like yesterday. The time just keeps flying by."

They walked back to the table. What Amir didn't realize at first was that when they hugged, Michael had slipped the flash drive into his jacket pocket.

They sat and talked for a while. Michael told him of the work he had been doing for the last month, and how the vice president was testing his loyalty and putting him through the wringer emotionally.

"I don't envy you," Amir said. "Right now, where you are is the last place I'd want to be. I don't believe I could handle the job you're doing. I don't know how you're holding up."

"I think what keeps me going is I keep thinking about my father. Maybe I'm somehow trying to avenge his murder. I can't wait for this to be over. I feel like I'm on a roller coaster that has no end in sight."

"From what I hear on my end it may take another year or more to complete. We can't lose sight of what we're doing," Amir said. "Hey, I'm starved. Let's eat. And, when the check comes, don't reach for it. Lunch is on me. Well, actually on the company."

"Too bad I don't like caviar, as long as you're buying, I would have ordered the Osetra at $180 an ounce. It would be worth it to see the look on Moslek's face when you hand him the lunch check." They both laughed.

Their server came over to take their drink order. They both ordered iced tea and said they were ready to order lunch. Michael ordered first.

"I would like a cup of your lobster bisque to start, and then I'll have your Top Shelf Cheese Steak. Could you make that with Swiss instead of provolone?"

"No problem!" She turned to Amir. "What can I get you?"

"I would like the same, but I'll keep the provolone, and instead of the soup, a chopped house salad. Thanks."

The server picked up the menus and left.

Michael looked at Amir and said, "When I hugged you before, I dropped a flash drive in your left jacket pocket. Don't look at it now. It's for Ian. Make sure he gets it. It's the legislation that's going to Congress in about a week. I want him to be aware of what's coming down. Melat wants it passed before the next recess."

"What time do you have to be back at the office?"

"I don't. He told me to take the rest of the day off. By the way, he sends his regards."

"Yeah, give him a big kiss for me when you see him next." They both laughed.

They finished their lunch in about forty minutes and sat for another half hour drinking coffee and reminiscing about school. "Do you realize we've been sitting here for almost an hour and a half? What time is your meeting?" Michael asked.

"In about twenty minutes, but fortunately it's only about three blocks from here."

Amir signed the check, which had been sitting on the table, and took his copy of the receipt as they got up together to leave. As they left the restaurant, they hugged once again. "Let's not be strangers. It's nice talking on the phone, but let's get together once in a while," Michael said.

"I promise."

Amir turned left and walked off as Michael turned right and walked up 9th Street NW. After crossing over New York Avenue toward the Historical Society, he took a seat on a bench in Mt. Vernon Square and called his mother. "Hi, Mom."

"Hi, Michael. How are you doing?"

"I'm fine, Mom. I mean physically I'm great. I still work out and eat the right foods when I can. Remember I told you Amir was coming to town? We just had lunch together. He looks great and is doing well."

She could tell from his voice, which sounded half-hearted, that something wasn't right. "Michael, what's wrong? I can hear it in your voice."

"Mom, I'm having a little bit of a tough time emotionally."

"Why, my son?"

"Mom, you know what the day after tomorrow is." It wasn't a question. He knew she knew.

She confirmed that with, "Yes I do, Michael."

"He would have been sixty. I miss him so much."

"I know, Michael. So do I."

CHAPTER 37

It was no surprise when the legislation prepared by Michael for the vice president was presented to the House before the Thanksgiving recess. Because of the cooperation that was prevailing within corporate America, it was easy for him to convince Congress to overturn the legislation that had stood for over 125 years. The vice president was certain he had more than enough votes.

The repeal was approved by a large margin, mainly because it had the stamp of approval from President Amanti, who had the respect of both parties in Congress. His private meetings with the vice president and the leaders of both houses were more than convincing for them to go ahead with their approval.

The vote was 298 to 127, with six members abstaining and four absent. One week later the Senate concurred with the House by a vote of 74 to 26 without a single amendment.

Without government monopoly regulation, corporations were now free to do as they wished when it came to mergers and acquisitions. Within thirty minutes of the passing of the bill, John Malcom, a member of the inner circle of the Samson and Delilah Society, received a phone call from a private number. The voice on the other end of the line simply said, "All roadblocks have been removed. It is time to move forward."

He was certain it was the vice president. He called Ian and told him the amendment had passed. "Now we have our work cut out for us. We'd better get started."

Everything seemed to be falling in place.

Over the next twenty-two-months the global corporate world was in an upheaval like a runaway freight train with endless track, fueled by corporate mergers and acquisitions. One by one, companies were bought and sold, not in a spirit of corporate greed but in one of consolidation as competitors became one.

The Dow Industrial stock index closed out the end of the summer of 2029 at 25,921, a new record high. The 100th anniversary of the stock market crash of 1929, which had begun a worldwide depression, came and went with no one paying attention to the date. The economy was extremely strong. Corporate profits were higher than ever before.

Oil was down from a high of $148 a barrel during the summer of 2008 to $28 on the latest commodities index, lower than it had been in 2003. It might have had something to do with the fact that the United States was now the leading exporter of crude oil since opening up drilling in Anwar, Alaska, off the Gulf Coast, and in the shale of Colorado, and since approval of the Excel Pipeline after President Obama left office. The U.S. now controlled over seventy percent of the world's oil.

Refueling a car since the repeal could be done only at the new name in town: Moexaco Sun, a combination of Mobile, Exxon, Amoco, Sunoco and BP. The price was a $1.55 for regular and $1.65 for premium; prices that had been unthinkable just ten years earlier.

A United States deficit was nonexistent, the budget was balanced, taxes were at an all-time low, and unemployment was at a record low at less than four percent. Corporate profits were at a record high. You could throw a dart at the Wall Street Journal, pick a company to invest in that way, and still would reap the rewards. Home ownership was at a record level. There were more millionaires living in America than ever before.

It was not much different in the European Union, the Pacific Rim nations, and the rest of the world. This newfound growth in the world's economy was credited to the peace accord between the United States, the European Union, the Pacific Rim Nations, and the Islamic Union of former terrorist nations.

Most of this effort was credited to the U.S. State Department working with its European counterparts to negotiate an international economic accord; which insured that corporations weren't fighting each other for market share. Everyone was happy with what they had; and what they had was plenty.

American corporations were becoming large conglomerates as they merged with their European counterparts. Although they were bigger and more profitable than ever before, their final retail products were manufactured so that they were affordable to all citizens of the world.

It really had started back in 2008, when there was a larger-than-usual number of mergers and acquisitions in corporate America and the world. In 2007, Saudi funds purchased 4.9% of Citi-Group. No one was paying attention as Sharia-compliant financing started to come to America. By the year 2014 an additional $1 trillion entered the corporate markets. However, the increase in corporate takeovers really gained momentum after the Anti-Trust Legislation was repealed. It was mergers and acquisitions on steroids.

The European Union companies as well as companies in the Pacific Rim nations weren't immune either, as the new wave of corporate mergers progressed. A financial news commentator once joked that if the consolidation continued, soon there would only be fifty companies listed on the New York Stock Exchange.

Halliburton merged with Schlumberger, and Toyota became the only name in vehicle manufacturing in the U.S. and Europe. In the U.S. they owned General Motors, Ford, and Chrysler. Harley Davidson was the only motorcycle you could buy. The names Suzuki, Yamaha, and BMW no longer existed.

If you wanted to fly domestically in the U.S., the only airline that could get you to where you were going was United Am-West. This was the new name for the merger between United, American, and Southwest airlines. Jet Blue, Delta, U.S. Air, and all other U.S. carriers also carried the new logo on their fuselages. The only manufacturer of airplanes was the Boeing division of General Electric, which also owned Airbus.

Movement of freight, either by rail, ship, or plane was completed by one company: Moslek Logistics, run by CEO Steven Moslek. All utility companies were under one name. All electric and gas bills were returned to the same lockbox for processing.

Although it might have been expected that all this consolidation of major corporations would create monopolies that would upset the balance of competition around the world, which did not happen. The cooperation between industries was unheard of. The economy of the world was on a tear, and there was no end in sight.

The amazing fact was that the corporations were putting back a good portion of their profits into keeping the infrastructure of the cities and towns up to date and in repair.

Since the terrorist-sponsored nations had agreed to lay down their arms years before, the need for large military budgets was diminished. Military operations were reduced to support services for natural disasters such at earthquakes, forest fires, and storms.

The global warming prophecy came and went, as the climate stabilized naturally, helped along by the 146 new nuclear power plants that were now operating around the world. The world was experiencing a new prediction as the climate changed naturally and produced a new concern: global freezing.

But, as cold as the world was feeling, it was heating up in the Middle East with Faheem's demands.

CHAPTER 38

The day after President Amanti left for the G-20 Summit, the vice president invited Michael to his residence for lunch and further discussions on all the corporate mergers and acquisitions. After lunch they moved from the dining room to the living room. Michael felt dirty once again, a feeling he had every time he was in the presence of Melat. However, he kept his composure and hid his real feelings. He knew he had to choose his words carefully, which he had been doing with composure, a style that had become easy for him as time went on. He had continually build up Melat's trust in him to the point that he needed him to be at.

"Michael, remember when we discussed the Twelfth Imam's return?"

"Yes sir, I do."

"What if I told you that it is about to happen? What if I told you that there is a plan in place to give the Twelfth Imam a path to return and lead the world in total and everlasting peace?"

"I would say that it would be an incredible task. How can that happen?"

"It can and it will happen. Michael, I am about to take you into my confidence and reveal to you a plan to create worldwide peace that will allow for the Twelfth Imam to return and walk among us in the name of Allah. What I am about to reveal to you must never leave this room. I want you to know that after sometime within the next six months, the world as we know it will never be the same again. Do I have your promise that in the name of Allah you will not reveal to anyone what you are about to learn?"

He looked at Melat trying not to show his disgust for him. "You have my word."

"Michael, you know that the mission of the Samson and Delilah Society is to control the world economically?"

"So I was led to believe. But I always thought of it as conjecture."

"Not anymore. The plan is real. I am telling you now that it is about to happen, which will pave the way for the Twelfth Imam's return."

"How can that be?"

"It is true, and you have unknowingly been a part of it."

"How is that possible?" he asked trying to sound surprised.

"When you helped to write the legislation to void the Sherman and Clayton Anti-Trust Acts, the passing of that bill helped opened the door for complete corporate takeover of the global economy. That was the last piece of the puzzle needed to complete the plan. The European Union and Pacific Rim Nations also relaxed their regulations after the U.S. did and allowed for an unprecedented amount of mergers and acquisitions to take place." Barry Melat was animated and jovial. It was like he had just hit the lottery.

He continued. "You know that all the members of the society are true believers of Islam. They are the CEOs of all these new conglomerates and know that the only way to have real peace in the world is for the total population to convert and become believers in Islam. Right now, as you and I are sitting here, the plan to convert the population of the world to Islam is being presented to the leaders of the G-20."

He then spelled out the plan that was being presented by President Faheem at the conference in Riyadh. Michael felt even sicker. He wanted to vomit, but with great difficulty he controlled himself. He had a mission to fulfill and didn't want to reveal his true emotions.

"What makes you think all the countries will go along with this plan?"

"They have no choice. We control everything they need to sustain themselves. It is either our way or nothing. It has been written, and it will be done."

He sounded like a madman. Michael knew he had to keep up his deception, but at the same time wanted to see what Melat was made of. He looked the vice president in the eyes and said, "You know my father was a true believer. He died when I was a boy. I wish he could have been here to witness this happening." Looking for some sign of emotion from Melat about his father, he saw nothing. How cold-blooded could this man be, he asked himself. "I guess I will just have to live the dream for him."

The vice president now felt sure that Michael was a true believer and could help carry out his plans with him. "Then I can count on you when the time comes? We will do it in the memory of your father. Michael you don't know how proud of you I am. You have become a true Mujahidin; a real warrior for our faith."

Michael's hatred of this man was intensifying. He was repulsed by him. He believed if he had a gun in his hand he could empty it into Melat's chest, turn around, and walk away.

"I promise you when our mission is complete you will be celebrated and rewarded beyond belief, Michael."

"Isn't that what everyone wants?"

"Yes it is. Come, let us pray."

The vice president removed two copies of the Qur'an from a bookshelf in his den and handed one to Michael. "Kaaba, the House of God, is in this direction. Let us pray for guidance."

Both men knelt side by side and faced east towards Mecca. Michael prayed the Qur'an with the vice president once again. However, the words that came from his mouth did not match what was in his heart and mind.

CHAPTER 39

A t 31,000 feet, President Amanti sat at his desk aboard Air Force One and glared at the leather-bound book in front of him. He hesitated, as he reached for it, the words of Charles Dunning of Great Britain echoing in his mind. "Please let us be smart about this. Let's leave this place and realize that we may have been complacent in some way by letting ourselves and our governments be lulled into believing that these people could be our friends."

Complacent, he thought. *How could we have been so complacent? Where did we go wrong? Was the world so caught up in the economic euphoria that we may have ignored telltale signs? Was no one paying attention over the past decade?* The questions were spinning in his head, like a toy top whirling on the floor with no apparent destination, hurtling against furniture and walls.

He reached for the book tentatively and removed the leather strap that was holding it closed. Opening it to the first page titled, "Instructions for the United States of America," he felt distressed. Turning the page he read on. "The following tasks will be completed within 180 days, or your country and all its territories will suffer great despair." The following text started with a letter to him.

"To the President of the United States: Your country has always assumed they were the leaders of the world. That assumption will soon come to an abrupt end as we now control almost every industry in the world. I can assure you that under the following plan the citizens of the United States will endure no harm or distress if you submit to our demands. The following pages will outline our demands, and we hope that you will adhere to them within the established time constraint of 180 days."

He tried to convince himself that this was one big nightmare. But how could it be? The CEOs of the largest and most important industries were there praying in Faheem's mosque. The first few pages laid out the plans for converting the American flag to the Islamic one. The words read like a laundry list of things to do. They included all the items that Faheem had spelled out in his warning to the members of the G-20, and then some.

"Your citizens will be told that they have nothing to fear, that Islam is a religion of peace, and no harm will come to anyone who acquiesces. If they resist and protest, it may be necessary for you to declare martial law during this phase of the conversion.

"Your Congressional and Senatorial leaders will immediately resign. They will be replaced by district imams, who will have complete control over each congressional district, led by a chief imam of each state, who will replace your current governors.

"The U.S. Constitution will be suspended, and all amendments will be declared void. Sharia Law will be the new constitution.

"Your gold reserves will be turned over to our treasury. The new currency of America and the rest of the world will be the Dinar, which will be backed by all the gold reserves of the world.

"There will be only one prayer book in your country, the Qur'an. All bibles and books referencing other religions will be removed from all your libraries, hotels, or other institutions they reside in.

"Your military will be suspended, and all weapons and armaments scrapped."

As he read the list, his heart sank. He wanted to scream but tried to remain calm. He was seething. He asked his chief of staff to call Charles

Dunning and Chancellor Gephardt on a secure conference line on their planes. "I want to speak with them privately.

When they got on the line he asked, "Have you read Faheem's demands?"

"Yes," was the answer from both. It took only a few minutes for them to realize that the demands were the same. "What are we to do?" Gephardt asked.

"I am not sure. We must remain calm until we have had a chance to digest his demands," Amanti said, his voice heavy as though it was hard to speak. He cleared his throat, then continued. "Who does this maniac think he is?"

"As I said before we left," Dunning said, "I think we should be careful whom we inform of this until we are certain who can be trusted in our own governments."

"I believe you are correct," Gephardt responded.

"Yes, I concur," the president echoed. "Let's be careful and try to formulate a plan amongst ourselves before we take any drastic action. We do have six months. I suggest we divide the list of those leaders who were present and inform them of what we just discussed. Let's try to plan a conference call in a week's time. Good-bye gentlemen. God be with us."

President Amanti picked up the binder from his desk and placed it in a file drawer. He locked the drawer and placed the key in his jacket pocket. As he did, he felt the note he'd been slipped earlier by Ian Sellers when they shook hands. In all his confusion he had forgotten about it until now. Unfolding it, he read the words that seemed to have been hurriedly scrawled on it. They simply said, "Nothing is what it seems." The note was signed, "Ian." He stared at the note for what seemed like hours, confused at its meaning.

CHAPTER 40

Three days later as he sat in his office alone, reading Faheem's demands for the fifth time, the intercom on his phone beeped. "I have Mr. Sellers on the line for you," his secretary said.

With apprehension he picked up the phone. "Ian, what in..."

Before he finished the sentence, Ian asked. "Mr. President, are you alone, and is this a secure line."

"Yes, I am alone, and no, the line is not secure. Should it be?"

"Please, sir, secure it."

The president pressed a button on his phone console. The call was interrupted for about ten seconds while the system was setting up the secure link between the two phones. After that, everything was encrypted. Encrypting a call inserts noise into one end of the conversation and removes it from the other. If anyone was listening in on the call, all they would hear would be static noise.

"Okay, we're secure. Ian, what in God's name is going on? Is this maniac for real?"

"I am afraid so, Mr. President. We must talk. But not on the phone. Let's meet where we can talk in private. We have much to discuss. As I said in my note to you, nothing is what it seems."

"If it weren't for your note, I would have had you arrested for treason," he said emphatically. "What is that supposed to mean—nothing is what it seems?"

"Please, Mr. President, in due time. All I can tell you are two things: No matter what you believe or saw, I am not part of this conspiracy, and second, I am certain it could be stopped. Just pick a private place to meet, and I will be there. But it must be just the two of us. This meeting must be completely private, with no one in earshot or visible."

"Why should I trust you?"

"Because it is your only hope to stop this zealot. We have been friends too long. Please trust me."

The president knew he had to explore all options. He was at his wits' end and muddled. He didn't have a plan, and as of now no other members of the G-20 had one either. At this point he was left with no choice but to hear him out.

"Okay, when do you want to meet?"

"The sooner the better."

"How about Camp David? We can meet here on Thursday. Marine One will take us the rest of the way. You can stay overnight if you wish."

"That's fine, but, not from the White House. There are too many eyes. How about Andrews? We can meet there."

"That sounds fine. I will see you on Thursday—let's say about two. I'll clear you at the gate."

"I know it's customary for a Marine in full dress uniform to meet you when you land and salute you. Please make sure no one is there to greet us. We must keep this meeting top-secret. Which also means your pilots must be sworn to secrecy, as well as your house staff."

"Fine! I will take care of that."

"One more thing: Please call the other leaders and tell them to sit on their hands until we talk. It is imperative to do it this way."

CHAPTER 41

They boarded Marine One for the sixty-six-mile trip from Andrews Air Force Base to Camp David, where they arrived about 3:00. After settling in, both men met in the living room, where many foreign dignitaries had gathered before.

President Amanti started the conversation by saying, "Ian, I am totally confused and more than a little apprehensive about this situation, which is leaving the leaders of the free world in a precarious position. I don't like it and frankly don't know what to make of it."

"I totally understand the position you have been put in. But you must believe and trust me when I say that everything is going to work out for the best."

"So you want me to believe that you, the CEO of the largest telecommunications company in the world, knows better than me, the president of the United States, how to combat and defeat this madman's ultimatum?"

"That's exactly what I am saying. What I am about to tell you is extremely confidential and so secretive that it must never leave this room. I need your word on this."

"You have it for now, Ian. But it will be conditional unless you can convince me otherwise."

"Okay! Let me tell you how this whole scenario came to be. It was the vison of the former grand imperial imam, Ahmed Samu, who devised a plan to take over the world by controlling the global economy. About fifty years ago, after the Iranian hostage situation ended, he formed a secret society known as the Samson and Delilah Society. The money they accumulated was from control of all the drug cartels and the profits from artificially inflated oil prices over the previous two decades. Once they had enough cash reserves, they let the price of crude drift back down. Over the past few years they let the U.S. believe they were the oil barons of the world, only they secretly controlled it all."

"I thought that Samson and Delilah was a fictitious group. It was always rumored that it existed but could never be proven," Amanti interjected.

"No! It really does exist. I am a member and have been for close to twenty-five-years. About two years after I became a member of the society, Samu died after a long battle with leukemia. Years before he died, he put a plan in place and groomed another individual take over his mission and continue in his absence. That person is a member of the Samson and Delilah Society and now has a very powerful position in your government."

"Who is it?"

"Not yet. Let me finish, please. Through the society, people have been groomed to become some of the most important business leaders in the world. Over the years they have become CEOs of and control almost every industry in the world. There have been mass consolidations of companies to build monopolistic industries. At the same time these companies became extremely community minded, so that the corporate world would no longer be looked at as selfish and only after profits. This was done to lull everyone into a false sense of security. The only way this plan would work was to assure that all members of the society were believers of Islam. Now that it was accomplished, there was only one thing left to do: Present his demands to the leaders of the world and complete the mission of the imperial imam Samu."

"So you are telling me that all the CEOs of these companies are under the control of this one person? Is it Faheem? One more thing, Ian: Are you a believer of Islam?"

"No and No! They believe I am, but I am not a believer, and Faheem is basically a puppet, but a powerful one. His task is to see that the mission is complete. Once it is in place, the real enemy will appear. And it is believed the Twelfth Imam will appear, as it is written in the Qur'an."

"And you know who this person is?"

"We are absolutely certain."

"You keep saying we, Ian. Who is 'we'? Why do you keep saying 'we' and 'our'?"

"For now I cannot say. Please, you must trust me and what I am saying. This madman can be defeated, but it has to be on our terms."

President Amanti had so many unanswered questions in his mind. He was running on overload and felt as if his head would explode from stress.

"You tell me you have a solution and want me to trust you, but you can't divulge your plan to me. You won't tell me who this 'we' is. I am supposed to trust you on blind faith? After what I witnessed last week in the mosque and heard from Faheem's lips, you want me to put the fate of the United States and the entire free world in your hands? I am the president of the most powerful nation in the world, and you want me to let you lead us through this so-called valley of death? I would have to be insane, and you are insane for asking it of me."

Addressing the president by his first name, Ian asked in a soft voice, "Robert, how long have we known each other?"

"Over twenty years."

"I have always had faith in you. I have helped you with all your campaigns and positions in government. Our families spend holidays together. We have always been there for each other, in good times and bad. I am asking you to have trust in me and what I am saying—the same trust and confidence that I have had in you all these years. I will never do anything to hurt you or my country. You have to believe that. Just by being here with you, if this meeting were to be discovered by the wrong people, not only would my life be in danger, but my family's lives as well. I would never let anything happen to them. I would die first," he said with a sadness in his eyes.

"Ian, you have to understand my position. This is the most devastating political event that has taken place in the history of the world. If this maniac gets away with this, it will destroy life on this earth as we know it."

"You don't believe I know that? That is why I implore you to please let us handle this the best way we know how. We will defeat this madman, but it has to be on our terms."

At this point President Amanti believed he was left with no other option. He was about to throw caution to the wind. He kept thinking to himself, *Just because I know this man over twenty years, do I really know him?* His mind was running on overload. However, one thought kept haunting him: *"You know who your enemies are. It is your friends you have to watch."* Was this the case with Ian Sellers, or was he a totally sincere friend? *Do I really know him, or has he been deceiving me all these years? I only pray I make the right decision.*

"Robert, I am about to tell you something you may find hard to believe. But I swear to you every word of what you are about to learn is the truth. No matter what you believed or no matter what medical evidence showed, Vice President Karlin did not die of natural causes." He repeated to him what Michael Haman had previously learned from Leon Ahren in Israel.

"He was murdered. Murdered, so that the person who is leading this conspiracy could move into place and control what they believe is their destiny, as it is written in the Qur'an."

"Murdered! I find that hard to believe."

"It is true. He was given a very powerful drug, which when ingested causes the heart to stop beating. This drug disappears in the tissue of the body and evaporates through the pores as fast as alcohol. It is untraceable by any scientific means."

"I find that extraordinarily hard to believe."

"Believe me, it's true. His removal was needed to make room for the architect of the conspiracy to move into position, so he could eventually become the leader of the most powerful nation in the free world: the United States."

"Ian, you must be insane," he said with skepticism. "That sounds like a Hollywood script.

"It is not, Mr. President."

"Are you telling me that this person is someone in America and will be running for President with a guaranteed win and take over the U.S.?"

"No, I am telling you he is already in place, and only one heartbeat away—yours! Part of their conspiracy is your elimination if you don't acquiesce to their demands."

"Are you trying to tell me that Barry Melat, a man I have trusted and loved for as long as I have know you, the vice president of the U.S., is the leader of this madness?"

"We have no doubt. He and Faheem are the leaders of this conspiracy."

Robert Amanti sat there in shock as he tried to process what he had just heard. His head was spinning as though he were on a twisting amusement park ride and could not get off. "How do you know all this, Ian?"

"Because they believe that I am part of the conspiracy. We also have people very close to him, whom he trusts. People in his administration who are very close to him are keeping a watchful eye on him for us."

"Who would that be?"

"I believe you know them: his legislative assistant, Michael Haman, and Secret Service agent Ron Moss. Please, Robert, I implore you, everything you just learned from me must stay within the four walls of this room."

"You have my word, Ian, but can he be stopped?"

"We have a plan. I promise you it is foolproof. However, you and the other leaders must let us proceed our way. I know we can stop this madness."

"If you have all the proof, why don't I just have him arrested and stop him?"

"It's just not that easy. He has others who are involved who will carry it through. Let us take this to the end."

"Are you sure? Nothing is one hundred percent."

"I know, but I promise we won't fail."

Robert Amanti, the most powerful leader in the free world, was about to relinquish control to a friend whom he had no choice but to believe in. He thought to himself, *What if I am being taken for a fool? The entire free world will depend on my decision.* "What is your plan, Ian? I must know it before I say yes and call the other members of the G-20."

"Here is what we want you and the rest of the G-20 nations to do: nothing!"

"Nothing! You really are insane! Nothing! What do you mean, nothing?" He was shouting as he paced the room.

"Just what I said. Let the time expire. It would be impossible to stop everything he has threatened immediately. It would take time to accomplish. Although they are in this together, Faheem is second in command, followed by a progression of other conspirators. He is currently Melat's puppet and takes his orders from him. However, he will move into the top position if anything happens to Melat. That is why you cannot arrest him. It will only accelerate their plan. I promise you this, once they lift a finger it is over. They will be defeated."

"You want me to speak to the other members of the G-20 and tell them to do nothing," he said sternly, as if to admonish him for his suggestion.

"Yes! You have to convince them it is the only way to defeat these people. They also must be cautioned to trust no one in their governments."

I don't know any other way to prove to you that Melat and Faheem can be defeated before he begins. It is not that simple for them. It will take some time. They can't just throw a switch and turn everything off. If after the time runs out we fail, have me arrested for treason and execute me. It won't matter. My life will be worth nothing at that point anyway."

"Those are harsh words, Ian."

"I mean it, Robert. If that's what it takes to convince you, so be it."

President Amanti believed at this point he had no other choice. There didn't seem to be any other options. "Then I will make the call."

"One more thing, Mr. President. Only one person should communicate with Faheem. This way there will be no confusion as to who is in charge. You should be that person. Faheem should not be influential to any other member of the G-20. You have to be the one who speaks for the group in its entirety. But realize that anything you tell him will go right back to Melat."

"Agreed!"

The next morning, after a restless, sleepless night and early breakfast, President Amanti called his secretary to arrange a phone conference with the members of the G-20 on a secure line. With the exception of the Far East and Australia, it was still daytime, and most everyone would be alert and able to be on the call. It took about forty-five minutes to get the leaders together on a secure conference call.

The president explained what Ian Sellers had expressed in the plan. Most seemed reluctant to proceed the way Amanti wanted to. He knew he had to sell this to them like his life depended on it, because it did. "I was skeptical at first but soon realized that we can't just start making plans individually to stop him in our own countries. We have to defeat him completely. We must cut off the head of the snake."

The members listened intently as he told them of the Samson and Delilah Society and how it all played into a master plan to control the global economy. They seemed astonished at what he told them.

"You mean to tell me that this Samson and Delilah thing is for real?" Gephardt of Germany asked.

"Absolutely it is."

Dunning asked, "You want us to trust you on the say-so of a friend?"

"I have full faith and confidence in him. We have been friends over twenty years. He is one of the most powerful business leaders in the world, and I believe everything he has told me." A small part of him was in doubt, but he couldn't let it cloud his judgment. There seemed to be no other way.

Jacques Frisse of France asked, "Does anyone else have a plan, because I don't. I haven't had a night's sleep since I returned."

There were no responses to his question. "Then I don't believe we have any other choice. I just pray we are doing the right thing," the Frenchman added.

"Gentlemen, I will inform China, Australia, and the other members when it is a decent time to call them," Amanti said. "One more thing, gentlemen: It is imperative that if any of you hears from Faheem, he is to be referred to me. I must be the spokesman for all of us. May God bless us all."

The call ended. President Amanti turned to Ian Sellers and said. "Don't make me regret this, Ian."

"You won't, Mr. President."

CHAPTER 42

President Amanti returned to the White House and resumed his position as the most powerful leader in the free world. However, he was filled with fear and anxiety. *What if Ian's plan fails?* He kept asking himself. *How do I face my people? What about our friends and allies in the rest of the world? How could we all have been so preoccupied that no one saw this coming?* The questions played over and over in his mind. And the most important one: *How do I continue to conduct the business of my government for the next six months with a heavy heart, knowing that the possibility exists that the world as we know it may change forever? But I have to go on.*

There were 169 days left for the nations of the free world to maintain their status as democracies.

Would democracy prevail, or would the world now become a global dictatorship?

He wanted so desperately to confront Melat but knew he couldn't. He didn't want to give him any indication that he knew of his involvement. He hadn't seen the vice president face to face since returning from the G-20. He was unsure if he could look him in the eyes. But he had to; he had to keep up appearances. There was so much that needed to be done to conduct the daily business of the country that required his interaction with the vice president. Amanti knew he had to wear his mask well.

CHAPTER 43

One week before the deadline, Ambassador Salaam Mamet of the Union of Islamic Nations telephoned President Amanti. "Mr. President, His Excellency Faheem wanted me to remind you that he has not received an answer to his request."

Request! He calls this a request, he thought to himself. *What balls!* "Tell his Excellency that I and the rest of the G-20 are still considering it. We will have an answer for him by his deadline." His heart was heavy as he knew he had relinquished all control of the situation to Ian Sellers. The clock was ticking fast.

It was less than twenty-four hours before the deadline was to expire. The leaders of the nations that made up the G-20, with the exception of the Islamic Union, met on a secure conference call. Prime Minister Dunning started the conversation by asking if everyone was prepared, in the event the United States' plan failed. The members stated that they had assessed the situation and knew what inventories their countries had as far as food, water, and energy supplies that were on hand. They each knew how much time they had before they ran out of supplies. They realized that in a few short days they would know if Ian Sellers' plan would work or not. They had time to reconsider.

"I only pray that this friend of yours knows what he is doing," Frisse of France said.

"I have full faith and confidence in him. I know his plan is much larger than that of Faheem's," Amanti stated. "Tomorrow I will call Faheem and tell him what our decision is. May God be with us all."

The following morning Robert Amanti called Faheem and stated to him in one sentence, "On behalf of the United States of America and the other members of the G-20, we categorically reject your demands."

"Then you will begin to suffer the consequences. One way or another you will acquiesce, either on your own or by force." Faheem was astounded. He thought he had them where he wanted them, and they were dismissing him like a piece of gristle cut away from a steak. "You leave us no choice. Good day, Mr. President." Faheem hung up. "How arrogant," he said aloud as he pounded his fist onto his desk in anger. "They will pay for their insolence."

Within fifteen minutes the secure line in the vice president's office rang. It was Faheem for Vice President Melat. "Your president and his friends have rejected our demands. Shall we proceed?"

"Yes. Start with their fuel supplies. I will handle communications and the Internet from my end. After one week, if that doesn't demonstrate how serious we are, then we will shut off the rest of what they need to survive. I have stockpiled enough food and water in my home to last for at least eight months. I am certain I won't need that much. This should only take a few days for them to succumb."

"It shall be done. May Allah be with you."

"And you as well."

Faheem called Peter Omar, the CEO of Moexaco Sun. "The other members of the G-20 have rejected our demands. It is time to proceed with our plans. Stop all shipments of natural gas, diesel, and gasoline immediately. I will notify the other members of the society of their decision, so they will be ready with our response."

"Yes, your excellency. I shall handle it immediately."

At the same time the vice president telephoned Ian Sellers. "Ian, it appears that your friend the president and his friends around the world have rejected our demands. It is time for us to show them how serious we are. Faheem is notifying Peter Omar to stop all oil and gas shipments immediately. Starting tomorrow morning, I want you to shut down all telecommunications and Internet service to everyone in the G-20."

"Consider it done."

"If they don't believe we are serious by the end of the week, water and food will be next."

Omar sent out an email to all the super tankers, oil barge operators, and oil depots to stop shipping fuel immediately and to shut the pipelines for all natural gas deliveries with the exception of their own regions. One by one, giant oil tankers went dead in the water to await further instructions. Tanker trucks returned to their depots to stand idle.

It took about three days for filling stations to start feeling the lack of supply. Within a week, fuel was rationed. Only emergency vehicles were allowed to receive fuel. Natural gas supplies were limited to what was in their holding tanks.

Fights broke out at filling stations as people demanded to be served. Cars were stranded on the streets and the sides of roads as they ran out of fuel. Public transportation that relied on gasoline and diesel came to a halt. Bicycles suddenly became the primary means of transportation.

People grew angrier by the minute as they demanded their governments take action. Yet they did not know why deliveries were being halted. News stations only speculated on why there were no deliveries of fuel.

At the end of week one, as suddenly as fuel had stopped being delivered, the water supply of the countries, cities, and towns stopped flowing. Food deliveries stopped, and air and rail transportation came to a grinding halt. All the provoked governments declared martial law. However, military personnel refused to report for duty because they had their own families to care for. Crowds gathered in the streets. All banking operations ceased, and ATMs no longer worked.

Within two weeks after the food supplies ran out, riots and looting were rampart. The shelves in every store were all picked clean. People had begun to kill farm animals for nourishment.

Riots were spreading to government buildings everywhere as people demanded answers.

The only lines of communications that were open were government news stations. Leaders finally told their citizens why all supplies needed to maintain daily life were being suspended. It didn't take long for people to demand that their governments surrender and fly the enemy's flag.

Hunger, thirst, and the want of supplies for sustainable life are great motivators for surrender.

CHAPTER 44

I an Sellers called Michael. "How are you holding up?"

"I'm fine. I'm not sure about the vice president. He is extremely angry and confused. He has been on the telephone constantly with Faheem. How are you doing?"

"Good. We are getting ready to finalize our plan. I have called Leon Ahren. He and the prime minister are ready to meet with Faheem as soon as he gets a call. I am meeting with the president today to tell him how we will finalize our mission and put some order back into the world. Michael, I know what is about to take place next will not bring your father back, but hopefully you'll be able to find some justice in what we have accomplished."

Ian Sellers entered the Oval Office carrying a large cardboard file box. As he placed it on the coffee table between the sofas, President Amanti rose from his desk, walked toward, him and hugged him. "Thank God, Ian!" Nothing more had to be said.

"Mr. President, these files contain all the evidence you will need to complete our plan. I ask only one thing of you before you proceed."

"What's that, Ian?"

"It would be nice if Michael Haman could be present during the final phase. It would mean a lot to him."

"I don't see why not."

"How much more time do you believe we will need before everything is in place? The way things are proceeding, I believe we can wrap it up by day's end. The prime minister is on his way to meet with Faheem as we speak. As soon as he surrenders, they will start air lifting food and necessary supplies to the victims."

"Ian, I don't have to tell you that the past six months have been the most frightening and stressful in my life. There was a time that I was starting to doubt you and the members of your society."

"I can understand your apprehension. But we knew we had to control the situation our way, in complete secrecy. It was almost forty years in the making, but we managed to make it happen. Perhaps now there will finally be absolute peace in the world; a just and authentic peace."

"Yes, Ian, I believe you are right."

"Mr. President, have you spoken to your counterparts in the rest of the world?"

"Yes, I have. When this is over, Frisse of France wants to award you the Legion of Honor. Charles Dunning of England wants to bestow the Knight Grand Cross on you and wants King William to bestow knighthood on you. Gephardt of Germany has asked that all those nations involved sign an endorsement for you to receive the Nobel Prize for Peace. I don't have to tell you that the U.S. Presidential Medal of Freedom will be yours."

"Mr. President, I am flattered by all these gestures but must humbly decline. This was not a one-man effort. Hundreds of people working in closely guarded secret together made this happen. There were no weak links in our chain. I was only the leader of the group; this was a group effort. No one person was responsible for bringing this to a peaceful conclusion."

"Your humility is overwhelming, Ian."

"Thank you, Mr. President."

Ian's cell phone rang. As he answered the call, Robert Amanti listened to his side of the conversation and heard him say. "Yes, that is wonderful news, Mr. Prime Minister. I am with President Amanti now. I will relay the message to him." He disconnected the call and once again turned his attention to the President. "Faheem has accepted Israel's terms. The Israeli Prime Minister suggests we proceed on our end and put the final nail in their coffin."

"Then let's take care of business."

President Amanti called his secretary and asked her to send in the FBI director and Ron Moss.

When both men entered the office, the president asked them to remain behind the door to his private study until it was time for them to reappear. Ian left to wait in the outer conference room out of sight until he was needed.

He then called Vice President Melat and asked him to come to his office with Michael for a brief meeting. Within two minutes, Vice President Melat and Michael Haman entered the Oval Office. President Amanti asked the vice president and Michael to have a seat on one of the sofas. He sat on the opposite sofa facing them.

The president spoke sternly. "Melat, I want to tell you that I know what you have been up to and what your conspiracy was." He consciously spoke in the past tense because he knew the threat was over and there was only one more thing to do.

"I have no idea what you're talking about," Melat answered. He tried to act surprised.

"Don't give me that crap. We've been on to you for years, you and your little secret society," Amanti said angrily.

"I really don't know what you are talking about. What secret society?"

Michael had all he could do to control himself and not smile. He sat there and listened to the president intently.

"I know everything about your plans, and the Samson and Delilah Society, and how you intended to take over the world. Don't try to bullshit me." He was seething. He wanted to grab Melat by his throat and choke the life out of him. "You're trying to tell me that you haven't been acting like the puppeteer and pulling Faheem's strings."

"Robert, I have no idea what you're talking about," he said while glancing at Michael as if to tell him not to say anything.

"Don't call me 'Robert.' That is reserved for my friends. To think I trusted you all these years. We were inseparable. I treated you like a brother. I helped nurture you and bring you along in your career. I even had your name put in nomination for secretary of state. When the big moment came, I asked you to join my team as vice president. We were going to change the world for the better. Only now I discover you want to destroy it. So don't call me 'Robert.' I am your president, although where you're going, you won't need a president, and you certainly will not have any friends. The gallows are too good for your kind." He was shouting and having trouble monitoring his anger, but knew he had to maintain his self-control. With that said, the president asked Michael to have his secretary tell the person waiting in the outer office to come in.

Michael left the office and returned a few seconds later with Ian Sellers. When he sat down this time, Michael was in an armchair perpendicular to the sofas. Ian sat next to the president.

The vice president looked stunned when Sellers entered the room. He seemed paralyzed in fear of what might happen next. Now he was bobbing in the middle of the ocean without a life jacket, and nothing to grasp onto to save himself was in sight.

"Ian, would you please tell Arbry Tamel what we know." The president referred to his second-in-command by his given name and not the alias he had been using since college.

"Who is Arbry Tamel? My name is Barry Melat. I'm Barry Melat," he repeated as if to convince himself. The vice president seemed shaken and started to get up from the sofa. *I can't believe I have been exposed*, he thought to himself. He was frightened and wanted desperately to run out of the room.

"Sit down, shut up, and listen. All the doors to this room have been locked from the outside. You are done. Unless you want to jump through the windows, there is no way out. Now shut up and listen." Turning to Ian, he said, "Tell him what we know."

Ian began. "You were born Arbry Tamel, a U.S. citizen. Your parents died in a horrible traffic accident when you were eighteen. Only it wasn't an accident. It was a murder arranged by Ahmed Samu, the imam you worked for as a muezzin. He knew your parents were suspicious you were becoming radicalized. He and his people needed to eliminate them so they could have complete control over you."

Tamel seemed shocked when he heard his parents had been murdered, but he tried to cover up his feelings by saying, "That's preposterous. My parents died in an auto accident."

"Believe what you want. We know different."

It was obvious that Tamel was becoming agitated. He had a look on his face like a child who had shown up in school without his homework. Any minute he was going to be discovered. Only it was too late, his teacher already knew he wasn't prepared. And Melat/Tamel wasn't prepared for what was coming next.

"Four months after your parents were murdered, you traveled to Indonesia to continue your radicalization. When you left Indonesia and returned to the States, you took on a new identity orchestrated by your leader. Your birth name, Arbry Tamel, was changed through a surreptitious operation. Every document that had your name on it was changed to reflect your new identity. From your birth certificate to your school records, driver's license, voter ID, and everything else, it was all altered to reflect your new identity by some of the best forgers in your little circle. The two things they couldn't change were your fingerprints and your DNA. We have both. We know your true identity. There is no denying it."

"That's a lie. I love my country."

"Which one?" President Amanti interjected, angrily.

Ian continued, "The Samson and Delilah Society was set up by your chief imam Samu's predecessor. They wanted to recruit the brightest business minds who were believers of Islam. Their mission was to radicalize them in a peaceful manner to take over corporate America and corporate Europe, and bring the Far East into the mix. It might have worked except for one thing. The greatest intelligence service in the world, the Israeli Mossad, who is responsible for intelligence collection, covert operations, and counterterrorism, caught on to your scheme from its beginning."

They noticed that Tamel was becoming even more agitated and fidgety.

"You believed that the covenants of your Qur'an *taqiyya and kitman*, which called for religious deception, whereby a Moslem could pretend to be a Christian, Jew, or any other religion to convert the world to Islam would work to your advantage. Well, we took that covenant and used it to our advantage."

"Who is 'we'?" Tamel asked.

"Almost all the members of the Samson and Delilah Society, including myself, are members of the Mossad. We are all Israelis with MBAs and PhDs in economics, pretending to be Moslem.

We took your Qur'an and turned it against you and your people. The religious deception you so proudly speak of is what we used. We did what radical Islam does, only we pretended to be Moslems. We used your money from oil and unfortunately illicit drugs to our advantage. You thought your money was being used by Moslem companies, when all along it was Israelis pretending to be believers of Islam. We could have shut you down anytime we wanted to. But we needed to defeat you completely and bring religious sanity back to the world."

Tamel started to feel sick. He felt like the room was spinning out of control. He tried desperately to regain his composure as Sellers continued.

"Once you made your demands through Faheem at the G-20, you believed that everything was going to be in place to complete your plan. We let your conspiracy play out. The only ones who knew what you were planning were the members of the society. None of the other world leaders knew what we knew. It was my task to convince them to let us take it to the end and defeat you."

Tamel's mouth felt dry like cotton. "Can I have a drink of water?"

The president walked over to a credenza that had a small refrigerator built into it and retrieved a plastic bottle of water for him. He was afraid to give him a glass for fear he might shatter it and cut his own throat. All other glass objects on the tables next to and between the sofas had been removed earlier for the same reason. Ian let him take a drink, then continued.

"The rest you already know. When you gave the order for Faheem to shut down all services and necessary supplies to live on, you expected America, Europe, and the rest of the G-20 members to immediately succumb to your demands.

"What you didn't count on was it backfiring on you and your people. We shut down everything as you demanded, except we shut it down to all the Arab nations. We didn't do it to hurt your citizens. We did it to make sure there would be an everlasting peace in the world. That was everyone's peace, not just an Islamic peace. Religious diversity has been the cornerstone of the entire world since the beginning, and that is what we wanted to preserve.

"The last item in your demand was that all countries must fly the Islamic flag and convert to Islam. Let me tell you what is happening as we sit here. The prime minister of Israel, Adam Cohen, and his delegation are delivering tens of thousands of Israeli flags that will now fly throughout all the Arab nations, on all government buildings, all public transportation vehicles, and anywhere else an Islamic flag is flown. They will remain there until Faheem accepts our demands, which are very simple. Our six-point plan is as follows:

1. Faheem will resign and will face criminal charges. He will be publicly tried in the International Criminal Court.

2. All Islamic nations will recognize the State of Israel and its right to exist.

3. All the nation members of the Islamic Union will hold free and open elections.

4. Twenty percent of your treasury each year will be deposited in a fund to educate your youth about world religious history in a truthful manner—not the rhetoric that radical Islam has been teaching about the Jews and Christians being devils.

5.   You will never be asked to convert your mosques to synagogues or churches. You may continue to practice your religion as you do. However, if any people in your countries want to practice Christianity, Judaism, Buddhism, or any other religion they desire, they will be allowed to do so in peace, without interference from your governments or ayatollahs.

6.   The women of your nations will have the same rights as the male members of your countries.

This universal doctrine is being delivered to Faheem as we speak. Once he signs it and steps down, everything in the Arab world will return to normal, but it will be a new normal. Do you understand?"

"Yes!" he said sheepishly. "What happens to me?" he asked the president, his lips quivering.

Robert Amanti opened a file folder that was on the coffee table between the sofas and removed a letter. He slid it across the table to Talem, handed him a pen, and said, "This is your letter of resignation. Sign it. It is effective immediately. You will then be arrested for treason and the murder of Alan Haman, Michael's father. You will be tried and, if convicted, which I have no doubt you will be, you probably will be sentenced to death in accordance with the law.

"Do you have any other questions?" Amanti asked.

"No!" Talem leaned over and signed the letter.

President Amanti proceeded to his private study, where Moss and the FBI Director were sequestered and asked them to come in. "It is time," he said.

The two men entered the room. Noticing Ron Moss, Tamel asked, "You are part of this too?"

"Yes! I have been watching you for years. What I am about to do gives me great pleasure. Stand up," he ordered.

Facing him he said, "Arbry Tamel, also known as Barry Melat, you are under arrest for treason against the United States, under Article Three of the U.S. Constitution and for the heinous act of conspiracy to commit murder against Alan Haman."

Moss continued to read him the Miranda warnings of his right to counsel.

After Tamel acknowledge he understood his rights, Moss reached for his handcuffs and ordered Tamel to turn around and place his hands behind his back. As he stepped forward to place the handcuffs on him, he hesitated. Turning to Michael he asked, "Would you like to do the honors?"

"It would be my pleasure," Michael answered as he took the steel restraints from Moss and snapped them shut on Tamel's wrists. The ratcheting sound of the handcuffs echoed throughout the room.

Moss and the FBI director, holding on to his arms from both sides, walked Tamel out of the Oval Office. He was trembling, his head bowed cowardly as they walked the corridor toward the elevator, to the astonishment of the West Wing staff. He was sobbing uncontrollably, as tears streamed down his face, a man in despair and defeat.

EPILOGUE

One month after Faheem signed the Israeli doctrine and relinquished his position, the Samson and Delilah Society disbanded. Its secret would be known only to those in membership and a select few. Each person knew that the evidence of its existence would be taken to their graves.

Michael Haman was named as the assistant to the president for economic studies. Before he took on his new duties, he flew to Israel with his mother and became a bar mitzvah. Amir, Ian Sellers, and Leon Ahren attended the ceremony, which was held at the Western Wall in Jerusalem.

Ian Sellers set up a perpetual scholarship fund in the name of Alan Haman, to be used to help underprivileged students who were proficient in business pay for college.

Three weeks after his arraignment in court, Arbry Talem was found dead in his cell. He had hanged himself by braiding a makeshift rope out of his bed sheet.

Four months later, on the anniversary of the death of Joseph Karlin, Ron Moss traveled to Connecticut to visit his old friend's grave. There was a second gravestone that had appeared two years earlier; it was that of Anne Tavis Karlin, the late vice president's wife. They were both resting at peace together.

Moss placed a bouquet of flowers on each grave as he had done every year since the passing of the vice president. He then recited the *Kaddish*, an ancient Hebrew prayer recited in honor of the dead, which praises God and expresses a yearning for the establishment of God's kingdom on earth. He wanted to pay tribute in his own way to a man and woman he had learned to respect and love.

As he stood there, a light snow started to fall, just as it had on that fateful day twelve years earlier. Moss reminisced about the events of the past years and how he knew that Joseph Karlin was sacrificed to open the door that allowed people to be moved around like chess pieces on a board to defeat Talem's plan so the world could live in religious harmony. Joseph Karlin had given his life so that a true and everlasting world peace could exist. Moss's heart was heavy, and he knew what he had to do.

Two days later he was back in his office, packing up his personal belongings. He shipped them to his ex-wife so she would have something to remember him by. He then wrote a letter of resignation from the Secret Service and placed it in the mail.

The next day, Ron Moss, former Secret Service agent, one of the only members of the Samson and Delilah Society, besides Michael Haman and Arbry Talem, who was not a member of the Mossad, walked into FBI headquarters and confessed to the murder of Joseph Karlin.

ABOUT THE AUTHOR

Michael Solomon is a former NYC Police officer and the recipient of 19 medals for meritorious and exceptional police work. As a member of the Intelligence Division, Michael has walked with presidents, monarchs, world leaders, the homeless, and the meek.

After 15 years of police work, Michael entered the corporate world of finance and management. Admired by his peers and subordinates he then struck out on his own and became one of the most successful small business owners in his field.

Following his personal success, Michael's charitable work earned him the respect and praise of his community. In 2003, he was honored by the New York State Senate and Assembly as Humanitarian of the Year in a distinguished resolution.

He has written Guest Editorials for national trade magazines and has also been the subject of numerous magazine and news articles. He has appeared as a frequent guest on over 350 radio and television shows as a political and business analyst.

After his retirement in 2003 he began his writing career with two bestselling non-fiction books. *"Success By Default-The Depersonalization of Corporate America,"* and *"Where Did My America Go?"*

"The Conversion Prophecy," is his first novel. It won't be his last. He currently lives in Florida and does business consulting, political and motivational speaking on a national level.

CPSIA information can be obtained at www.ICGtesting.com
Printed in the USA
LVOW06*0830251015

459644LV00001B/3/P